Praise for *F. E. Higgins's*

The Black Book of Secrets

A 2007 *Booklist* Editors' Choice
A Book Sense Top 10 Title for Winter 2007-2008

★"A smart, peculiarly thrilling book that is sure
to appeal to readers ready to sidestep the
goody-goody Harry Potters of adventure fiction."
—*Booklist*, STARRED REVIEW

★"This polished debut from a British writer tantalizingly
blends secrets and thick, evocative atmosphere. . . .
Original and engrossing."
—*Publishers Weekly*, STARRED REVIEW

"Strongly seasoned with details of nineteenth-century
oddities, the story abounds with puzzles,
quirks, and enticing disclosures."
—*The Horn Book Magazine*

The Bone Magician

F. E. Higgins

PUBLISHED BY

FEIWEL AND FRIENDS

NEW YORK, NY

Y
FICTION
HIG

A FEIWEL AND FRIENDS BOOK
An Imprint of Macmillan

THE BONE MAGICIAN. Copyright © 2008 by F. E. Higgins. All rights reserved. Printed
in the United States of America. For information, address Feiwel and Friends,
175 Fifth Avenue, New York, N.Y. 10010.

Library of Congress Cataloging-in-Publication Data

Higgins, F. E.
The bone magician / by F. E. Higgins.
273 p.
Summary: With his father, a fugitive, falsely accused of multiple murders
and the real serial killer stalking the wretched streets of Urbs Umida, Pin Carpue,
a young undertaker's assistant, investigates and soon discovers that all of the victims
may have attended the performance of a stage magician who claims to be able to
raise corpses and make the dead speak.
ISBN-13: 978-0-312-36845-6 / ISBN-10: 0-312-36845-3
[1. Mystery and detective stories. 2. Magicians—Fiction. 3. Undertakers and
undertaking—Fiction. 4. Dead—Fiction.] I. Title.
PZ7.H534924Bo 2008   [Fic]—dc22   2008006777

First published in the United Kingdom by Macmillan Children's Books,
a division of Pan Macmillan.

Feiwel and Friends logo designed by Filomena Tuosto

Designed by Barbara Grzeslo and Scott Myles

First Feiwel and Friends Edition: September 2008

10 9 8 7 6 5 4 3 2 1

www.feiwelandfriends.com

To Andy
Η μεγάλη βλακεία είναι θάνατος

—Anon.

"And none could rival the Beast in its ugliness"
Anon., "The Tale of the Hideous Beast," from
Houndsecker's Tales of Faeries and Blythe Spirits

Boane magycke—anciente praktise of raiysing deade
bodyies

Jonsen's dictionary, c. 1625

A Note from F. E. Higgins

When we last met, I was snowbound in Pachspass, the ancient mountain village where Ludlow Fitch and Joe Zabbidou had such trouble in *The Black Book of Secrets*. While I waited for the thaw, intending to follow in their footsteps, I uncovered the seeds of another story in a city to the south. Its name was Urbs Umida and I soon realized, with a mixture of delight and trepidation, that this must be the selfsame "City" from which young Ludlow had fled his evil ma and pa.

Hardly altered by time, the River Foedus flows silently as ever through the heart of the Urbs Umida. The north side has flourished, but the south side is practically abandoned. After three days of searching, using what sparse clues I had from Ludlow's memoirs, I found the narrow alley where Lembart Jellico, Ludlow's good friend, had kept his pawnshop. To my surprise, the shop was still standing and occupied, by a Mr. Ethelred Jelco, who dealt in antiques. It was he who sold me the exquisite wooden box containing the battered remnants of Pin's Journal and the articles from the *Chronicle* wherein I first read of Benedict Pantagus and Juno.

The Bone Magician is neither a sequel to *The Black Book of Secrets* nor a prequel. It is what I like to call a "paraquel." The events in this story took place at the same time as the adventures of Joe Zabbidou and Ludlow Fitch in Pagus Parvus. To read this story it is not necessary to know what came before, but perhaps after this you will want to go back to find out.

As ever, it is not my place to advise you, only to reveal to you what I know.

F. E. Higgins
England

The Bone Magician

Pin's Journal

How I have come to hate this place of evil, this city of nightmares. Urbs Umida they call it, Dank City, and well it deserves its name. It has taken everything that was precious to me. But I shall leave one day, soon, when I know the truth. I shall pass through those gates and it would please me greatly to not look back. Imagine, never again to inhale the stink of rot and decay, never again to see despairing eyes in the shadows, and never again to hear the name Deodonatus Snoad or to read the lies from his poisonous quill.

Fiends, but this place is cold. Winter marches on, the last day of February today. Ah, I can write no more, my fingers are numb. I want to sleep, to wrap myself in darkness. Sometimes I think that maybe _this_ is the dream and that soon I will open my eyes and everything will be the way it was. But then, when such small hope has dared to surface in my heart, I smell the river and I know that her stench is very real.

CHAPTER ONE

Strange Company

A corpse on the cusp of putrefaction could hardly be considered the most entertaining company on a winter's evening, but Pin Carpue didn't do what he did for the conversation. He did it for the money. Tonight, however, things were different. If the body he was watching—her name, when alive, was Sybil—had revived and tried to engage him in some sort of discourse, he couldn't have replied even if he had wanted to.

For Pin had just succumbed to a soporific drug.

Hardly able to move, certainly unable to speak, he lay in a semi-comatose haze on a bench in the corner of the dark room. The last thing his soggy brain recalled was leaving his lodgings. As for his immediate whereabouts, it was a mystery.

With a supreme effort Pin finally managed to open his heavy eyes. He stared into the gloom, but it was difficult to make any sense of his surroundings when he had double vision. His thoughts were like clouds floating in the sky, shapeless and gently moving. Overall, he decided, this feeling, this woozy buzzing between his ears, was not wholly unpleasant.

Somewhere in the room soft voices were whispering and, if Pin had allowed them, they would have lulled him back to sleep. But another part of him was conscious enough to know that he wanted to stay awake. For any other boy it most certainly would have been beyond his capabilities to keep his eyes open under such difficult circumstances, but Pin was used to staying awake until the early hours. It was part of the job.

The job of watching corpses.

He also had a powerful ally in his pocket, a glass phial, full to the brim with the waters of the River Foedus. It was a distasteful job, gathering her noxious liquid, but now he was silently thankful that he had filled it earlier. If he could only reach it! His fingers, usually nimble, were like soft rubber and he fumbled just trying to lift the flap of his coat pocket. Eventually he managed to grasp the phial and bring it out. He rested before he engaged in the next struggle, removing the stopper. His hand couldn't do it, so, with a tremendous effort, he raised the bottle to his mouth, though his arm felt as if it was moving through deep water, and pulled the cork out with his teeth. He took a long, deep sniff and immediately his eyes began to smart and the inside of his nose stung sharply as if he had bitten down on a mustard seed.

"Fiends," he exclaimed in his head and blinked. But the brew had the desired effect and a second sniff brought him slowly back to his senses. Thus slightly revived, though quite exhausted, Pin focused his mind on his situation.

Now he remembered where he was. This was the *Cella Moribundi*, the waiting room for the dead, in Mr. Gaufridus's basement. For some reason he had been drugged by those people, the three shadows that were moving around at the table in the center of the room. He did not think to try to escape, his deadened limbs would not have allowed it. Besides, he had a feeling that *they* were not interested in him but in the body lying on the table.

"He's waking up."

The girl's voice sent a shot of panic through Pin's veins. He could see a figure moving slowly toward him out of the darkness. Inside he was gripped with fear and tried to cry out, but he was unable. So he closed his eyes tightly. If she thought he was asleep she might leave him alone. He knew when she was right beside him. She smelt of juniper and the sleeping drug, aromas he would not easily forget. Pin felt her sweet breath on his face.

"Give him some more," instructed a man's voice.

"No, I think he is still under," she said finally. Then all was quiet.

Slowly, cautiously, Pin dared to open his eyes again. The waters of the Foedus and the lingering effect of the girl's drug were a potent combination, leaving him in a sort of in-between world. He noticed that the candles had been relit and, from the voices, he knew there was the old man, the girl,

and a younger man (he sounded like a southerner). In his present state there was little he could do. So he lay back to watch, wholly entranced, the strange drama that was about to play out in front of him.

CHAPTER TWO

Grave Matters

Only a few hours earlier Pin had been in complete possession of his senses. He left his lodgings in Old Goat's Alley after a small supper of ale, bread, and a piece of fish on the turn and trudged off through a shower of hail that was rapidly turning to snow. Pin was always glad to see the back of the place. Old Goat's Alley was considered the worst street south of the River Foedus which, if you knew what the rest of the streets were like, was a frightening thought. Whereas other streets might have a redeeming feature or two, perhaps a slight slope to allow the ever-present sludgy waters to flow away, or a more even distribution of potholes, there was nothing that could be said in favor of Old Goat's Alley.

The tall, narrow houses were poorly constructed, hurriedly built, and squeezed into any space available. The rooms had been divided and subdivided so many times that each house was labyrinthine within. This made it very difficult for the constables when chasing criminals. As did the numerous exits and narrow alleys behind the houses. The buildings leaned slightly forward, which gave cause for alarm if you looked up. It also meant that large amounts of snow slid off periodically into the street below. Few people did look up, however, weighed down as they were with their cares (and ever mindful of the pickpockets). Old Goat's Alley was badly lit, which made it a haven for every sort of criminal that existed. Some nights the lamplighter wouldn't turn up at all and although this was inconvenient for a few, it must be said that many inhabitants were happy to carry out their business in the dark.

As for the rest of the City, certainly on the south side of the river, most pavements were in a state of disrepair and the streets themselves were little more than a mire of noxious debris, churned up daily by the horses and carts that wheeled through and the herds of cattle, pigs, and sheep that were driven along on market day. Each evening the mire froze on account of the extreme temperatures that were currently being experienced. It was a winter like no other.

Barton Gumbroot's lodging house was toward the end of the alley. It was a filthy hovel which Barton had split into as many rooms as possible to maximize rental income. Pin was always uneasy about returning to his room, day or night. His fellow residents were without exception a strange lot and each had particularly nasty features or habits, often both. As for Barton Gumbroot, Pin wouldn't trust the man as far as he could throw him. It was well known that he practiced as a tooth surgeon, another lucrative profession, down in the cellar. Night and day everyone heard the shrieks but no one had the stomach to investigate. In fact, Barton had intimated on more than one occasion that he would take a tooth or two in exchange for a week's rent, but Pin had refused. All this and more was going around in Pin's head as he hurried along beside the river. Just before the Bridge he stopped at the top of a set of stone steps that led down to the water.

The rich really are different, he thought ruefully as he looked across the water. The Foedus was always a foul-smelling river, but the odor was hardly noticeable on the north side because of the prevailing wind. Thus even the air the rich breathed was better. From his vantage point Pin could make out the silhouettes of their fine houses. He didn't need daylight to know what they looked like: double-fronted with sparkling glass, fancy woodwork and glossy doors, polished brasswork and red tiles and frowning gargoyles.

And he knew what sort lived in them, the sort who spent their money on frivolous things, for idle amusement to alleviate their boredom. And this money was not worked for. God forbid that those perfumed men over the water with their frilled cuffs and silken breeches might have to do a day's honest toil. And as for their good ladies, with their noses in the air and their skirts so wide they couldn't fit though a door, well, by all accounts, daily they took their ease, drinking tea, drawing, and singing. No, their wealth in the main was inherited but that was no guarantee it was come upon honestly. Money wasn't the only thing the rich inherited. The duplicity of generations was in their blood. Perhaps they didn't commit the same crimes as took place nightly over the river—the rich liked to keep their hands clean—but they still stole from their fellow man and murdered, just in a more sophisticated way and usually with a polite smile on their faces.

It might be a fine thing to live over the river, thought Pin, *but I wonder, is it better to be in a beautiful house looking at an ugly one, or to be in an ugly house looking at a beautiful one?*

Yes, he thought, as he descended carefully to the sticky black mud below, life on this side was harsh and dirty and noisy, but for all its unpleasantness, there was an honesty of sorts among the southerners. You knew what they were from looking at them. They couldn't hide it beneath fine clothes and words.

The tide was out but on the turn. Pin made his way as quickly as he could to the water's edge. It was not unusual to find sailors' trinkets in the mud, fallen from the ships, but tonight Pin was in a hurry and wasn't looking. He took from his pocket a small two-handled glass phial and removed the cork. Holding one handle delicately between thumb and forefinger, he dipped it just under the surface and dragged it along until it was full of the dark water. Then he corked it carefully and ran back to the steps.

The smell of the Foedus was renowned far and wide but,

exposed to something on a daily basis, a person can get used to most things. It was a rare day in Urbs Umida that the stench was so bad people actually remarked upon it. There is a theory that over time native Urbs Umidians developed a sort of immunity to the smell. This theory might also account for their apparent ability to eat rotting food with impunity. If you can't smell it, you can't taste it. For Pin, however, this was not the case. He had a sensitive nose and was acutely aware of the most subtle changes in the river's odor.

By the time Pin reached the churchyard it was snowing heavily. He passed through the gates, head down, narrowly avoiding a young girl who was coming out. She held up her pale hands in fright. Pin caught the faintest scent as he brushed past her, sweeter than one would have expected, and felt moved to mumble an apology before going on through.

As a place of burial St. Mildred's was almost as old as the City itself. Like a bottomless pit, it held far more people below than was indicated by the headstones above. This was not as difficult as it sounded, for the earth was unusually wet and acidic. These factors combined to speed up the process of decomposition considerably. Given that the churchyard was on a hill, all these decaying juices seeped underground down the slope into the Foedus. Just one more ingredient to add to her toxic soup. It was not unknown for bodies to be skeletal within a matter of months—a phenomenon that was often talked about in the Nimble Finger Inn by those in the know.

But Pin wasn't thinking of rotting bodies as he made his way between the uneven rows of headstones. He walked purposefully until he reached a small unmarked wooden cross. It was leaning to the left and he tried to right it with some difficulty, for the earth was frozen solid. A small bouquet of dried white flowers, stiff with the cold, lay at the base of the cross and he picked them up before hunkering down in the snow.

"Well, Mother," he said softly, "I haven't been for a while, and I'm sorry about that, but Mr. Gaufridus is keeping me busy. I'm working again tonight. You know, I'd rather do that than spend a night at Barton Gumbroot's. He's a sly one, always asking about Father. Is he coming back? Did he really do it? I don't know what to say."

Pin paused after each question, almost as if expecting an answer, but none was forthcoming. So he sat there shivering, oblivious to the thickening snowflakes, turning the flowers over and over in his hand.

CHAPTER THREE

A Death in the Family

It was almost two months ago now, back in early January, but Pin still remembered coming home that night as if it was only yesterday. He knew as soon as he went up the stairs that something wasn't right. He could hear excited voices and exaggerated sobbing and when he reached the landing there was a small crowd gathered outside his room. He recognized some of their faces, the lady from the room next door, the chimney sweep from across the corridor, the wash erwoman from downstairs. When Pin saw the looks on their faces he felt cold fear. He pushed through the crowd into the room to see a lifeless figure sprawled on the floor in front of the empty fireplace. A stout man in dark clothing was leaning over the body.

"Father?" Pin's voice trembled.

The man looked up and asked officiously, "Are you Pin Carpue?"

Pin nodded.

"And is this your father?" He moved to one side and the face of the dead man was fully revealed. Pin swallowed hard and forced himself to look. "No," he said, "it's my uncle, Uncle Fabian. But I do not care for him."

"You're not the only one by the looks of things," said the man as he drew himself up to his full height and coughed self-importantly. He took out a small black notebook and a piece of charcoal. Pin now knew him to be Mr. George Coggley, the local constable.

"What happened to him?" asked Pin.

"Strangled, more'n likely," said Coggley. "His eyes are near out of his head. Where is your father, son?"

"I don't know," replied Pin cautiously. He looked around at the people all staring at him.

"If you know where he is, you must tell me, otherwise you'll be in trouble."

"Why?"

"Cos we reckons it's 'im what done this," chipped in the washerwoman almost gleefully. "'E was seen runnin' orf." She had never liked Pin or his father, the way they considered themselves above everyone else. As for his mother, who did she think she was, God rest her soul, coming over the Bridge to live here? There was no place for northerners on this side of the river. They just didn't fit in.

"Running away from the scene of a crime," admonished Constable Coggley. "He's our man."

"I knew he'd come to a bad end," muttered someone else.

"Allus the same wiv these people, ideas above 'is station, never done no one any good."

Pin stood in the midst of the mumblings and accusations, speechless and bemused. Right now he hated them all, with their sly looks and snide remarks. He knew what they thought of his father. It was as plain as the crooked noses and squint eyes on their ugly faces. Pin had learned early that he was different. The children on the street teased him relentlessly, because his mother was from a wealthy family, because she spoke with the soft vowels of the north and not the harsh grating voices of the southerners. But what they resented most of all was that the Carpues claimed to be poor, just like the rest of them. What nonsense, they exclaimed! How could a lady with such manners and airs not have money? And what other reason would Oscar Carpue possibly have for marrying her? It didn't help that Uncle Fabian kept turning up dressed in his finery (though his pockets were empty). Oscar had sent him away time and time again. "We have nothing for you," he said.

The torment had continued even after his mother's death the previous year. After that, people chose to resent the fact that Oscar Carpue wouldn't share his inheritance with his neighbors. "I have no inheritance," he told them more than once. "I'm only a carpenter. We're penniless."

But he never convinced them, and now Fabian was dead, murdered, and once again fingers were pointing at Oscar Carpue. Pin spent the next week scouring the streets day and night, but there was no sign of his father and no word from him. The week after that, Pin had to leave the lodging house. Not only could he no longer afford it on his own, but neither was he welcome. He spent ten miserable days looking for work, finally taken on by Mr. Gaufridus. Thus he was able to take a room at Barton's, though it was his greatest desire to leave there . . .

Pin shivered, brought back to reality by a large snowflake that landed between his neck and the collar of his coat. The quarter hour rang out and he jumped up.

"I've got to go now, Mother," he said. "I can't be late for Mr. Gaufridus or he will find another boy to take my place. He says there are plenty out there willing and I believe him. People will do anything for money in this city. I won't leave it so long next time, I promise."

He touched the cross lightly, then turned and ran quickly and nimbly through the graves and out of the churchyard, running all the way to Melancholy Lane, where he finally came to a breathless halt beneath a sign that read:

CHAPTER FOUR

Goddfrey Gaufridus

In a city where merely to be born was considered the first step toward dying, it is fair to say that Goddfrey Gaufridus, coffin maker and undertaker, had a relationship with death that was closer than most.

Although the business of undertaking was generally considered profitable (customers were guaranteed), Goddfrey hadn't always wished to deal so closely with the dead. At the age of fifteen Goddfrey was struck down by a mysterious illness, which rendered him incapable of speech or movement for nearly three months. He spent those three months lying on his back in bed. After a week his mother and father, realizing his was a condition that might be permanent, thought it best to carry on as normal.

Worn out by the torture of being able to do little other than think (and what thoughts he had in those drear months!) Goddfrey fell asleep one night and didn't wake up. By the third day his mother was quite convinced that he was dead.

She asked Goddfrey's father to the room and they stood over him for some ten minutes. "I believe he is gone," said Mr. Gaufridus, and they called upon their neighbor to confirm this, the physician being too expensive, and then arranged the burial.

As was often the case at that time, and luckily for Goddfrey, the undertaker proved to be rather less than honest; he quietly sold the boy's still unmoving body to the Urbs Umida School of Anatomy and Surgical Procedures and buried a sand-filled coffin. On the fifth day of his sleep, Goddfrey, fully rested by now, awoke to find himself flat out on the surgeon's table in an exhibition theatre. A shining scalpel was suspended above his head and the surgeon was just about to plunge the blade into his chest (strangely enough, it was the way the light reflected off the blade that made the greatest impression on Goddfrey and in later years similar flickering light brought back uncomfortable memories), and thus stimulated, Goddfrey summoned up every ounce of strength he had and managed to emit a whistle.

"I think your corpse is alive," shouted one of the audience, a medical student who had just further confirmed his reputation for stating the obvious. Goddfrey was taken home to his grieving parents who, failing to understand how he made the transition from the grave to the surgeon's table, nevertheless welcomed him with open arms. It wasn't exactly the journey they had thought ahead of him, but they preferred not to think on it for too long, and within a couple of days he was back to his old self.

Well, not quite. The strange disease had one legacy: facial paralysis. Poor Goddfrey had only limited use of his facial muscles with the result that his expression (sleepy) was now constant. He could neither smile nor frown, laugh nor cry—at least not in a way that was immediately obvious—and he could only speak through gritted teeth.

After his narrow escape at the School of Anatomy, Goddfrey was determined that what had so nearly happened to him would not happen to anyone else. He became an apprentice to the local undertaker and took over the business when his master died. Over the next few years Goddfrey Gaufridus gained a reputation as a man who could be trusted not to bury the living. This was chiefly because he put a great deal of time and effort into ascertaining that his charges were most definitely dead in the first place.

This might sound a little odd, but it must be remembered that in Goddfrey's day it was not as easy as you might think to determine that a person had actually departed this life for good. Apart from looking for breath on a mirror or listening to an often indeterminate heartbeat, there was little else a physician could do. Many times as he lay in his seemingly unconscious state had Goddfrey mused that if only someone had invented some mechanism, some sort of tool, that could indicate whether or not he was alive, then he would not have suffered as he did. He vowed that if he ever revived he would be that person.

So that is what he set out to do. But inventing and undertaking at the same time proved to be quite burdensome, so Goddfrey decided that he needed an assistant, and he put a small card in the window. Pin, by virtue of the fact that he could read—a skill passed on by his mother—was the only applicant for the job.

On the appointed day, Mr. Gaufridus took Pin on a tour of the premises. The shop at street level had on display both the most expensive and the cheapest of Mr. Gaufridus's coffin models, readily distinguished one from the other by the gloss or lack of it on the wood and the fittings. In a large double-fronted cupboard he kept a selection of goods available to hire for the funeral, including palls, dark suits, veils and black gloves, horse plumes, invitation cards for the ceremony, and a tray of funeral rings in the shape, naturally, of a skull.

Mr. Gaufridus then led Pin downstairs to a basement room where other coffins in a variety of shapes and sizes and colors, and at varying stages of completion, stood against every available wall. In the middle of the room was a substantial workbench, scattered with hammers, nails, lathes, and all manner of carpentry tools. The floor was covered with wood shavings and curls and sawdust. The walls were adorned with a huge array of brass and metal fixings, hinges, rims, nameplates, handles, and all the coffin paraphernalia you could think of.

All this looked perfectly normal to Pin and when Mr. Gaufridus led him to another room, he could not be blamed for expecting more of the same.

"Here we are," Goddfrey had said proudly, opening the door. "The *Cella Moribundi*. The waiting room of the dead."

Pin stood in the doorway and looked in. The concept of a *Cella Moribundi*, a room where the dead lay before being buried, was by no means alien to him or any other Urbs Umidian. It was a long-held tradition in the City, of now unknown origin, that a body must lie for three days and nights before burial. There was a saying in Urbs Umida: "If in doubt, see three days out." Pin thought back to his mother's death and the long hours he and his father had spent sitting with her corpse in their lodging house. They had not been able to afford Mr. Gaufridus.

The room itself was smaller than the workshop and considerably cooler. In the center there was a high table (vacant at that time) above which was suspended a peculiar mechanism consisting of strings and cogs, wheels and levers, and a recently oiled chain. There were numerous shelves and a set of narrow scientific drawers, displayed above which was a collection of what could only be described as instruments of torture.

"What on earth is all this?" asked Pin, looking around in amazement. This was unlike any *Cella Moribundi* he had ever heard of.

Goddfrey frowned, by which I mean his left and right eyebrows moved fractionally toward each other.

"All this, as you put it, is the result of years of work on my part for the benefit of the living and the dead."

Pin was hardly any more enlightened.

"Er, how?"

"My dear boy," said Goddfrey through his gritted teeth, "imagine the most terrible thing you can and then think how it would be if it was ten times worse."

Pin thought for a moment. "To fall in the Foedus and to swallow some of her water," he said with a degree of prescience.

"Hmm," murmured Mr. Gaufridus, "that indeed is a terrible thing, but can you imagine something worse?"

Pin could—it involved Barton Gumbroot—and he told him, but it still wasn't quite bad enough. Finally Mr. Gaufridus leaned close and supplied the answer, in the form of a question.

"Boy, can you imagine anything worse than being *buried alive?*"

Pin felt a shiver ripple down his spine and he shook his head. Mr. Gaufridus appeared not to be watching because he continued unabated, circling the table and waving his arms about in a manner that was at odds with his expression.

"Imagine waking from a peaceful sleep to find yourself in complete and utter darkness. You reach out for the candle that you know is on the table beside you, but your hand is halted in midair by something hard on every side. You try to move but you can barely turn over. Confusion sets in before the terrible realization that this isn't a dream, that you aren't in bed, but *in your coffin.*"

Pin's teeth began to chatter. The temperature really was

significantly lower in this room. Mr. Gaufridus, however, showed no sign of stopping. Not a trace of emotion was evident on his face, but his eyes seemed to sparkle. There is no denying that he derived a strange sort of pleasure from reliving in part the nightmare of his youthful ordeal.

"What agonies you would suffer, lying there, hardly able to move. Doubtless you would try to stay calm, to conserve the air, because you would still hope that someone was going to find you. But as the hours, the days passed by, you would realize that no one can hear your shouts, your screams, your sobs. Imagine knowing that only two fates await you—death by lack of oxygen or death by starvation. You would clutch at your throat, gasping for every breath. Then as the final hours went by, you would be gripped by hunger that can never be sated and by a terrible thirst that cannot be quenched."

He turned to Pin. "Tell me, can you imagine anything worse than that?"

Pin, convinced that Mr. Gaufridus must be planning to bury him alive, was backing toward the door.

"I . . . I can't," he replied.

"Good," said Mr. Gaufridus, "then you will understand why I have made all this. True, there are those out there who build coffins with alarms and bells and flags, but not I. It is too late to ring a bell when you are buried. The damage has been done, not to your body but to your head. I, Goddfrey Gaufridus, have addressed the real root of the problem."

"Which is?" asked Pin shakily, still eyeing this strangely cool character with deep suspicion.

"That a person should be dead before he is buried."

"Oh," said Pin. *So he is* not *going to bury me alive,* he thought, but it was little comfort.

Mr. Gaufridus continued. "You will, in the course of your employment with me, have to know how to use all of this apparatus." As he spoke he took Pin by the elbow and maneuvered him toward the table. "Perhaps you could oblige?" he said, and he helped Pin up and laid him down.

"This is one of the first machines I ever designed and I have to say I am very pleased with it." He pulled off Pin's boot and sock and slipped a ring of leather around his big toe and tightened it. Poor Pin, his suspicion now replaced by utter bewilderment, tried to raise himself up on his elbows, but Mr. Gaufridus, oblivious to his discomfort, pushed him back down.

"Do you think if you were merely asleep that this might wake you?"

As he spoke Mr. Gaufridus reached up and began rhythmically pulling down on the overhead handle. The cogs and wheels began to turn and Pin's foot started jerking violently upward in a terrible syncopation.

"It might," said Pin, raising his voice to be heard above the creaking hinges and the rattling of the chain. "But I am sure that I would have to be in a *very* deep sleep for someone to think I was dead in the first place."

"Hmm." Mr. Gaufridus was thoughtful. It was rare he had the opportunity to test his inventions on a live body and he intended to make the most of it. "Then let us try this," he declared. He opened a slim drawer in the chest behind him and withdrew a rather long needle with which he poked, quite firmly it must be said, the exposed sole of Pin's foot.

"Aaaarrrgh," shouted Pin, and he leaped off the table, forgetting that he was still attached to the toe-pulling machine. The result could have been catastrophic except that Mr. Gaufridus grabbed him before he could bring the whole machine down from the ceiling. Wordlessly, though tutting occasionally, Mr. Gaufridus extricated him from the tangle of leather and strings and chains. After that, Pin declined to take part in any more demonstrations, refusing the tongue yanker with a firmly closed mouth, and insisted that Mr. Gaufridus merely *tell* him about the equipment. Whether he was disappointed or angry, or even equivocal about the matter, could not be gleaned from Mr. Gaufridus's visage, but he agreed to Pin's terms and the two of them then spent the next hour examining all sorts of instruments and devices designed to ensure that the deceased was just that, and not sleeping or in a coma or drunk.

The devices were many and varied. It seemed that Mr. Gaufridus had run the gamut of pain-inducing practices that might be usefully employed to waken the dead. These stretched from the uncomfortable—toe pulling and ear tugging—to the rather more painful—knuckle whacking and shouting in the ear—to the unimaginably excruciating, details of which can be found in Mr. Gaufridus's book on the subject, *Dead or Alive?* (a few copies remain in legible condition). Even the waters of the Foedus were put to good use. When bottled they increased beyond recognition in strength and odor, and Mr. Gaufridus was quite sure that one whiff was enough to wake the dead. As he went from one invention to another, Mr. Gaufridus expounded his theory that a dead body should be lighter than a live one on account of the soul having left it.

"How much would a soul weigh?" asked Pin.

"A very good question, young man," said Mr. Gaufridus. "It is easy enough to construct a set of scales, of course, but to have a person on them at the exact moment life leaves their body, that is the difficulty."

Pin was confident by now that Mr. Gaufridus was just the sort of person to solve such a problem. By the end of the morning, despite his initial doubts, Pin had to admire Mr. Gaufridus's determination that none should be buried alive. It was a lofty ideal indeed. Mr. Gaufridus, encouraged by Pin's curiosity and intelligent questioning, was happy to offer him the job.

"Apart from watching bodies," asked Pin, "what else exactly will I be doing?"

Mr. Gaufridus thought for a moment. "All sorts, my dear fellow, all sorts."

And "all sorts" was a wholly reasonable description of Pin's duties. He spent his days toe pulling, sole pricking, and tongue yanking, not to mention fitting in coffin carpentry—the precision of his dovetail joints was much admired by Mr. Gaufridus—and even the sincere consolation of grieving relatives. By night, if there was a body to be watched, he lay dozing on the bench in the *Cella Moribundi*, contemplating the change in his fortunes, secure in the knowledge that he would not be disturbed. As the weeks went by, Mr. Gaufridus relied more and more on Pin to look after the day-to-day running of the undertaking business while he spent his time maintaining and constructing his elaborate machines. Pin even began to sense changes in Mr. Gaufridus's mood from the tiniest alterations in his expression.

Tonight, however, when Pin arrived, Mr. Gaufridus was merely tidying up and making ready to go.

"Your last night with poor Sybil," he said, indicating the door into the *Cella Moribundi* with a nod. "She'll be gone tomorrow."

Pin bade him good night. He listened until he heard the door to the street slam shut before crossing the room and stepping into the *Cella Moribundi*. He didn't mind the dead bodies really, there was little room for the squeamish in this city, and the benefits of actually having a job far outweighed the disadvantages. Granted Mr. Gaufridus's basement room wasn't the warmest of places—after all, dead people preferred to be kept slightly chilled—but it was better than being out on the street.

Southerners were quite happy to sit with their dead for the requisite seventy-two hours. In fact, they turned the three days of waiting into a sort of party in the dead person's honor. Northerners, on the other hand, considered this practice rather vulgar (not to mention inconvenient) so undertakers usually employed a fellow, in this case Pin, to sit with the corpse in their place. And of course, in some ways it was a measure of wealth that a family could afford to pay extra for this service. How they liked to tell their neighbors of the extra expense incurred by tongue yanking.

If by the third day the body still showed no signs of life, then it was considered safe to bury it. By then it was usually quite apparent in other ways that the soul was well and truly gone. Pin, with his sensitive nose, knew before most when a body was on the turn, so perhaps it was fitting that he should end up with such a job. There were benefits to having such a gift. A keen sense of smell enhances a dull existence. All the same, thought Pin, as he went toward his lifeless charge, in a city such as Urbs Umida, perhaps life would be rather less unpleasant if he had the sensory capacity of an ordinary mortal as opposed to that of a dog.

CHAPTER FIVE

Memento Mori

Sybil lay on a plump cream cushion on the table. Beneath the cushion a black velvet cloth hung to the floor, where it sat in soft folds. She was wearing a white floor-length gown knotted at the feet and pulled tightly around the neck. A scarlet embroidered sash was loose around the waist, and pinned to her left shoulder was a delicate glittering brooch in the shape of a butterfly. Her hands were clasped across her chest and she wore three rings on each hand. Her long dark hair was arranged to frame her pale face, and her head rested on a tasseled velvet pillow. Her eyes were closed, her long eyelashes brushing her cheeks, and her lips were red. There was no evidence of the parallel depressions across her body made by the cart wheels that had so cruelly ended her short life. Mr. Gaufridus prided himself on the peaceful look he achieved on the faces of his customers. He loved nothing better than to hear the words "She looks as if she is asleep" (even though, of course, he had made rigorous checks to ensure that this was not the case).

He was rarely disappointed. Those were in fact the very words the poor girl's family had uttered only two days ago when they saw her. Her mother had burst into tears yet again and all the while her father paced the small room, cursing the carriage that had run her over. He cursed even louder a certain youth, a Mr. Henry Belding, who had by some trickery managed to woo their daughter and entice her over to his side, the south side. Mr. Gaufridus had watched all this with an unchanging expression and a gentle consolatory murmur whenever he deemed necessary.

"How could it happen?" wailed her mother again and again. "My darling Sybil. So well brought up and yet she falls for such an unsuitable lad. His father was a street sweeper, his mother a gin seller. The shame!"

"Indeed," murmured Mr. Gaufridus. "I cannot imagine the distress it must have caused you. At least now you may take comfort from the fact that she is in a better place than with the son of a street sweeper."

Sybil's mother looked at him out of the corner of her eye, but Mr. Gaufridus was giving nothing away. Facial paralysis could be advantageous in his line of work.

Pin stood at the table and looked at the girl's peaceful face. The air was cool and he could smell the familiar aroma of death. It wasn't unpleasant; in fact the smells that Pin most associated with death were not human at all but the undertaker's herbal ointments used to preserve the skin. Pin was not a sentimental boy. In a city such as Urbs Umida, life was a gamble and death was a daily occurrence. It was an interesting equation: as you grew older your chances of living longer increased. If you could get past two years, then you had a good chance of making it to ten. If you could get through to fifteen, then there was a distinct possibility that you would make it into your twenties. And if you reached thirty, well, then old age was virtually guaranteed (old age commencing at forty and ending at forty-five).

Tentatively Pin reached out and touched the girl's hand; it was as cold as he imagined the deepest parts of the Foedus to be. She was young, no more than seventeen, and it saddened him. He was reminded of a line or two he had seen on a tombstone:

THOSE WHO DIE IN THE BLOOM OF YOUTH
TAKE BEAUTY WITH THEM TO HEAVEN'S GATE

Pin settled down on the bench. Sitting alone in the dark and chilly room, his thoughts turned again to his father, as they did most long nights. The whole Uncle Fabian business was a mystery. He knew what everyone thought, but he couldn't believe it of his father. And he wouldn't unless he heard it from the man's own mouth. Murderer? It couldn't be. Yes, it looked bad for Oscar Carpue. There was no denying the dead body left in his wake. But there was no proof. Only the locals, and Coggley, putting two and two together when half of them couldn't add. Pin had added it all up again and again and he reached the same conclusion every time. His father was innocent. But there was one little nagging fact. If that was the case, then why didn't Oscar Carpue come back?

"I shall think on it no more," he declared resolutely, and lay down on the bench with his hands under his head and tried to empty his mind of troublesome thoughts.

Pin snapped back to wakefulness from a light doze. The room was in complete darkness—the candles had all gone out—so he slid off the bench and went carefully to open the door. Someone was moving about in the workshop.

"Mr. Gaufridus?" he called.

Pin felt a rush of air and heard the sound of soft cloth flapping. As he opened his mouth to shout, a hand came around his face and pressed a damp rag hard over his mouth. He felt his eyes become heavy and his body go limp—and then nothing.

CHAPTER SIX

Pin's Journal

When I first began to keep this journal, at my mother's suggestion, I had not thought that I should ever make such a strange entry as this—to relate the events of that night with Sybil in the Cella Moribundi. I could see from where I lay on the bench that my unexpected companions were three in number, of varying heights, all dressed in dark clothing, two hooded, one hatted. They were not watching me so I decided to risk a third inhalation of the Foedus water. Just as I grasped the bottle, the young man at the table spoke.

"Are you sure he's all right, Mr. Pantagus?"

"Don't you worry, Mr. Belding," came the reply, and I saw the older man give the frightened fellow a reassuring pat on the shoulder. "The boy will be fine. Might have a headache later on, but that's it. He'll put it down to experience."

Mr. Belding, a youth of perhaps eighteen summers, seemed satisfied with this explanation. Besides, he had other interests that were more important than his concern for me. He turned back to the table and took the dead girl's hand.

"Poor darling Sybil, she's so cold." He sounded surprised.

"What did you expect?" muttered the girl, and I detected a nervousness in her voice. Mr. Pantagus looked over at her and smiled benignly. "Just relax, Juno," he said. "It won't be long."

I watched as Juno pulled at a thin string around her neck, but whatever was at the end of it I couldn't see, for she cradled it in her palm. Then she ran her finger under her nose leaving a smear, of some sort of unguent I supposed, across her philtrum. It shone softly in the candlelight. From the shine on Mr. Pantagus's upper lip I deduced that he had done the same thing.

"What's that?" asked Mr. Belding. "Do I need some?"

Juno shook her head and motioned to him to be quiet. In her right hand she held a delicate peardrop bottle on a silver chain. She began to circle the room slowly, swinging the bottle back and forth, back and forth, in a slow mesmerizing motion. As she passed, a smell as sweet as my own phial of Foedus water was acrid, and easily as powerful, drifted across to me. I inhaled it deeply, involuntarily. She continued on her way and when she reached Mr. Belding she stood behind him for a few seconds. As soon as he took in the perfume, he began to cough and sneeze.

"What are you doing?" he asked in a panic.

"It's merely a summoning potion," she said soothingly.

"I'm sorry," he whispered, "it's just I've never done anything like this before."

"Well, we have," said Juno gently. "And we must get on."

Gradually the whole room was suffused with the highly potent aroma. I watched intently through narrowed eyes as the girl took up a position beside Mr. Pantagus at the head of the body. Beneath her hood her pale skin was luminous in the candlelight. Mr. Belding waited anxiously at Sybil's side.

Mr. Pantagus reached into his cloak and pulled out a small drawstring bag. He loosened the tie and brought forth a handful of dried herbs, which he spread around the corpse's head, muttering audibly but unintelligibly as he did so. Then he reached into the bag again to withdraw a small pile of brown sticks. He crumbled them quickly between his fingers and scattered the powder along the length of the body. Some of the scents I knew—cinnamon and anise—but others were foreign to me.

Next he produced a wide-necked jar from up his billowing sleeve. He dipped his fingers into the dark liquid and flicked it about the room. The air thickened with the smell of artemisia and myrrh. By now I was reeling, even as I lay, from this aromatic assault on my senses. Young Mr. Belding, who seemed almost insensible with nerves and the heady aroma, watched the proceedings openmouthed, and all the while Juno stood back gently swinging the peardrop bottle.

Without warning, and with dramatic effect, Mr. Pantagus clapped his hands sharply. Even my dulled heart started at the sudden noise. Then he laid his hands on the dead girl's forehead, threw back his head, and began to speak from beneath his dark hood.

35

"I call upon you, Hades! Lord of the lower regions! Master of the shades of the dead!"

His somber tones sent a shiver up my spine and I trembled. Mr. Pantagus continued his exhortation.

"And your patient queen, Persephone, mistress of the seasons. Hear me, hear me now, and grant my request. Render unto us, for one brief moment, the very soul of this dead girl and allow this man to speak once more to his beloved."

His words hung on the chill air. Nothing happened. Then Mr. Belding gasped and took a step backward. And I too would have gasped had I been able, for Sybil, until now lifeless as a stone, began to stir.

A shudder went through Sybil's body from head to toe and she emitted a long whining groan. It made me want to cover my ears, but it would have been better had I covered my eyes. To my horror and astonishment the dead girl's eyelids flickered and opened. She turned her head toward Mr. Belding and a smile spread slowly across her face. I blinked hard. Could this really be happening? I watched, fascinated and disbelieving, but I cannot deny that what I saw felt very real.

Mr. Belding, with tears in his eyes, leaned over and spoke with incredulous surprise. "My dearest Sybil, is it you? Is it really you?"

"Yes, Henry," whispered the girl in a strangely husky voice. "It is I, your Sybil. Speak quickly, my sweet, we haven't much time."

The youth looked at Juno, who nodded to encourage him, and then he fell to his knees, his head resting on the table, and began to sob.

"You must forgive me," he said in a choked voice. "My last words were so cruel, spoken in anger. I cannot tell you how much I regret them. And before I could say sorry, that cart . . . you . . . you . . ." He faltered, brimming with emotion, then finished, ". . . were run over like a stray dog in the road." With an overwhelming sob he threw his arms across the body, his chest heaving and his shoulders shaking. He remained thus for some moments until Juno gave him a gentle nudge. "We do not have much time," she whispered.

Mr. Belding attempted to regain his composure. He wiped his nose with the back of his hand and smoothed his hair down on his head. He spoke haltingly.

"I'm sorry, Sybil, for saying those things I did. Please do not leave me to regret my harsh words for the rest of my life. I beg of you, tell me that you forgive me."

I had not thought it possible for a three-day-old corpse to smile warmly, but Sybil, as deeply moved by this entreaty as I was, did just that. She reached up to touch her poor Henry on the cheek.

"I forgive you," she said and then lay back on the cushion. The young man was once again in the throes of uncontrollable weeping and Mr. Pantagus threw a rather concerned look at Juno. She pulled gently at Mr. Belding's sleeve.

"It is over, we must go," she said quietly yet firmly. "It is fool-hardy to stay any longer. If we are found—"

"Of course," he said and hiccuped.

Mr. Pantagus opened the door and fresh cold air rushed in. Juno pushed Mr. Belding toward Mr. Pantagus, who pulled him through

the door. She made as if to follow but suddenly stopped in her tracks, crossed over to the bench, and stared right into my unblinking eyes. She was so close I could see an eyelash on her cheek. She smelt of juniper, I remember, but then she was gone.

CHAPTER SEVEN

A Good Profession

Juno stood at the tiny window that allowed the daylight into her room.

Not that there is much daylight in this city, she thought mournfully as she looked out at the purple and gray skies. Urbs Umida had been shrouded in night for hours now. The moon came out from behind the clouds intermittently but took cover again quickly, as if even she couldn't bear to look down on the city below. It was snowing again. Juno was aware of a whistling breeze from the badly fitting window so she closed the shutters and pulled down the wooden batten that kept them secure. Now the only light in the room came from the fire that glowed beside the bed and the two candles on opposite walls.

She took off her cloak and hung it on a nail in the back of the door, then went to the fire and held her trembling hands out to the flame. Several times she made as if to move but didn't, until suddenly, impulsively, she dropped to the floor, reached under the bed, and pulled out a small brown leather trunk. She fumbled with the buckles, but before she could open them a knock at the door made her jump. Guiltily, she pushed the trunk back before calling out, "Come in."

An old man looked around the door. His pallor was gray and his eyes were ringed with darkness.

"Benedict," exclaimed Juno, "you look terrible."

"Why, thank you," he said and laughed wheezily as he came to the fire and sat down on the chair. "It's those stairs," he said. "They'll be the death of me."

"Perhaps I can give you something. I have many remedies…"

Benedict's eyes darted over to the bed where the corner of the trunk was showing and he raised his eyebrows. "Thank you but no," he said. "There is no remedy for what ails me; there is no cure for the passing of time. And you, you rely on them too much."

"Don't scold," began Juno, but Benedict was seized by a coughing fit and spoke no more until it had passed.

"The weather has worsened."

Juno smiled. "Is that why you came up here? To talk about the weather?"

"No. It's something else. Something important."

"I think I know," she said quietly.

"I am not a well man, Juno. The time has come for me to stop all this traveling. It is beyond me. I have saved some money, enough for me to live reasonably well, and I have some for you too."

Juno shook her head. "I do not want your money."

"It is not mine," he said. "It is ours. You have earned it as much as I have, if not more." He laughed. "After all, where would I, Benedict Pantagus, humble Bone Magician and Corpse Raiser, be without my assistant?"

Juno was about to argue, but Benedict silenced her with a wave of his hand. "You could stay with me, of course," he said, but Juno could tell from his voice that he didn't think she should. "You are still young, though. You should leave this dreadful place."

"But what of Madame de Bona?"

"Take her with you," said Benedict. "She has served you well. It is a good profession. You can find someone else to help you."

"A good profession?" said Juno with a short laugh. "You really think so?"

"Do you not?" Benedict looked hurt.

"It's not you," said Juno hurriedly. "It's me. Our performances have been as successful as ever. These Urbs Umidians seem to have an insatiable appetite for Madame de Bona's predictions. It's just sometimes..." Her voice tailed off.

Benedict nodded his head. "I do understand. It's not an easy life, but don't forget, we, you, are giving these people something that is important to them."

"But some of them are suffering," said Juno. "They ask questions that pain them."

"And we take away their pain."

"I suppose."

41

"Do they not go away happy?"

Juno chewed her lip thoughtfully. "Yes, and sixpence lighter. Money they can ill afford."

Benedict looked at her and spoke softly. "People need relief, in whatever form. Sometimes I wonder how you will ever survive—you have such a soft heart."

"I don't think it is soft to be fair," Juno retorted, a little stung, not by his words but by the fact that he was closer to the truth than he knew.

"We have had this conversation before," said Benedict with finality. "We are neither tricksters nor pickpockets on the street. At least we give them something for their pennies."

Juno remained silent. Benedict eyed her carefully for a moment. "You know, Juno, I think you have other matters on your mind."

"Perhaps I have," she admitted. "And I think maybe it is time I paid more attention to them."

Benedict rose and took her hand in his. His knuckles were red and swollen and there were high spots of color on his cheeks. "If that is what you wish, I shall not stop you. Maybe I won't be with you, but at least let me help you. Take the money."

Juno smiled. "You have done enough. It was you who saved me from this city in the first place."

"And I could say the same about you. No matter. Think about what I said. You do not have to give up; it's your choice. Just consider it carefully before you make a decision."

Juno nodded. "Will you be all right?"

"I shall be fine after I have rested," said Benedict, deliberately misinterpreting her question. He went to the door and looked at her with a critical eye. "You should get some rest too. This city, it drains you."

He left and Juno turned back to the fire. Benedict had only told her what she already knew. He needed rest and good food and somewhere to stay for the winter. He wouldn't find anywhere better than Mrs. Hoadswood's lodging house. But the thought of staying in Urbs Umida made Juno's blood run cold.

"I have to go," she said determinedly.

She stood thus for some time deep in thought. In truth, Madame de Bona's performances were not so bad—certainly they could be considered entertainment—but the secretive corpse raisings, that was different. They made her very uncomfortable. She had not wanted to do Sybil's, but Benedict had persuaded her. She remembered the boy they had drugged. It was never her intention to hurt anyone. She couldn't get his eyes out of her head, one green, one brown.

She began to pace the room. A terrible struggle started up in her head. She took out the trunk again and placed it in front of the fire. She went so far as to unbuckle the straps, then she stood up and walked away, but her eyes never left it. At last with a cry of anguish she returned to it and flipped open the lid with shaking hands and took a deep breath as she surveyed the array of packets and pots within.

There were terra-cotta jars and waxed cotton bags,

stoppered glass bottles, soft leather pouches, and corked amphorae. She ran her fingers over the contents, then took out a small wooden pestle and mortar. Working quickly with a practiced hand, she sprinkled powder from one bag and crumbled leaves from another into the mortar. Next, she carefully added three drops of amber liquid and pounded the mixture into a paste. She scraped the paste onto a small burner and hooked it over the fire. Then she lay back on her bed and inhaled the sweetness and drifted off into aromatic dreams.

CHAPTER EIGHT

A Watery End

THE
GLUTONOUS
BEASTE

BETTY PEGGOTTY,
~~PROPPEYE PRUPTOR~~ OWNER OF

THE NIMBLE FINGER INN,

CANOT BE HELD RESPONSABLE FOR ANY ATTAK OF NERVES OR
APPOPLEXY OR ANY SUCH ILNESS THAT MIGHTE BE BROUGHTT
ON AS A RESULTE OF A CUSTOMER ENGAGING WITH (THAT IS,
OBSERFING OR SPEEKING TO OR FEEDING) THE GLUTONOUSS BEASTE.
ANY VISITER WITH A FRAIL CONSTITUITION OR A BAD HART IS
ADVISED THAT THEY STEP THROUGH THIS DOOR AT THEIR OWN RISKE.

IT MUST BE UNDERSTOOD THAT THE GLUTTONNOUS BEEAST IS A
MONSTROUS ABERRATION of NATURE
THAT MAY NOT BE TAMED
OR REASONED WITH.

ALL INQYREES TO BE DIRECTED AT ITS MASTER, MR RUDY IDOLICE
(TO BE FOUND ON THE CHAIR BY THE CURRTEN)

BY ORDER, *Betty Peggotty*

Harry Etcham was proud to be an ordinary Urbs Umidian, born and bred south of the Foedus, and well used to the smells and the filth and the ways of the southerners. He lived as many others did, surviving on his wits, his native cunning, and the odd—very odd—spell of honest labor. At the end of the day, he liked to take a drink or three in the nearest tavern, more often than not the Nimble Finger, which tells you as much about him as you need to know. Earlier that evening, on the recommendation of his friends and to satisfy his own curiosity, Harry decided to see the Gluttonous Beast for himself. After all, he had had what he considered a very successful day. Not only had he found two onions and a carrot that were still edible (by his standards), which he would add to his stew later that evening, but he had also managed to steal eight pennies from a blind beggar's hat. He was feeling quite merry even without a drink inside him.

Now he stood ponderously in front of the notice that was pinned to the wall. He proceeded to read what he could and understood enough of it to be confident that he was neither of bad heart nor frail constitution. As stated, the Beast's owner was seated close by on a chair, so he pressed sixpence into the man's hand and descended the stairs behind the curtain.

The smell that assailed him was almost choking and was certainly a match for the Foedus. Harry searched his pockets in vain for a handkerchief to hold up to his large nose but eventually resorted to his collar. The cellar was poorly lit, but by the time he had reached the last step, his eyes had adjusted to the dark. No more than three feet in front of him there was a barred cage. In the far corner he could make out a large shapeless figure. He listened carefully and could hear grunting and chewing and tearing and spitting. Then came a loud wet sneeze. To his disgust he felt droplets of spit, and he didn't dare think what else, spraying his face.

As he watched and listened he became aware that he wasn't alone in the room. Down one side of the cage, near the back, stood a man. He deduced this from the silhouette of his hat, for he was dressed in dark clothing and was quite formless and unidentifiable. His head was against the bars and he seemed to be whispering to the creature. Harry could not make out what he was saying, so he went closer but tripped over a stick and fell against the cage with a ringing thud. The mysterious figure started, and immediately hurried, head down, to the stairs, acknowledging Harry neither with a tip of his hat nor a greeting.

Slightly disconcerted by the man's rapid exit, Harry turned his attention once more to the cage. He could see him—there was no doubt in his mind that it wasn't a beast of the female persuasion—a little better now, but the Beast was oblivious to his presence and continued his grisly repast.

"Hey," said Harry halfheartedly. He hadn't paid sixpence for this. "Hey," he said more loudly. Still no response. He was looking on the ground for something with which to poke the creature when the Beast suddenly moved at light-ning speed from the back of the cage to the front and threw himself up against the bars. Harry found himself face-to-face with arguably the most grotesque creature he had ever set eyes upon. Living in Urbs Umida and moving in the cir-cles he did, Harry had seen more than his fair share of ugly creatures, but this surpassed them all.

The Gluttonous Beast opened his cavernous mouth and roared. His teeth were brown and yellow and spit dripped over his lower lip. His face was covered in hair and his eyes were bloodshot, with huge pupils. One of his hairy hands—or were they paws? Harry couldn't tell and he wasn't much interested right then—had a tight grip on Harry's collar.

"Aaaarrrgh!" yelled Harry as he twisted around and ripped off his coat and ran for his life up the stairs. He rushed through the curtain while the man on the chair opened one eye and watched him go with a barely concealed smirk. Rudy Idolice had seen all this before and it was good for business.

Outside on the Bridge, Harry stumbled across the pave-ment, only just keeping his balance by planting one foot heavily in the gutter. His foot sank ankle-deep in the thick sludge. He swore when he saw the state of his boot and then again as he felt the chill of the freezing water seeping in between the split seams and his laces. To add insult to injury, a cart drove by at a tremendous pace, the spinning wheels spattering him with filth. He gritted his teeth and flapped his shirt and trouser legs in a futile attempt to clean himself up.

He was sweating heavily and his stomach felt as if it was tying itself in a knot that was going to prove hard to undo. His head was filled with the sounds of the Beast. The slurping and belching, the crunching of bones. And the smell! "By God," he expostulated softly, and immediately his breath clouded around him. "That was some hellish stink."

The last time Harry had smelt something quite so repugnant was some years ago when for three high-summer days and nights the air in the city had stilled and the river had almost curdled.

He set off for home with that curious gait peculiar to all Urbs Umidians, instinctively mindful as they were of the crooked slabs and potholes underfoot. At least it wasn't snowing, he thought, and as he walked he was haunted with visions of what he had just seen. He breathed in a lungful of cold night air. "Lord above," was all he could say, over and over. To think that some people went to see the Beast again and again. *How?* he wondered. *Why?* But already he was considering it too. Could the Beast really have been so horrific? Perhaps he might go back, in a week or so, a few days maybe, just to see if his mind wasn't playing tricks . . .

With his head down into the sharp wind, Harry didn't

notice the man stepping out from an alley and falling in beside him.

"So you've seen it, then?" asked the man.

Startled, Harry stopped and looked up, but the moon chose that very moment to hide behind the snow clouds, and the next streetlamp was some distance away, so the figure beside him was as a shadow against a wall.

"Seen what?"

"The Beast," hissed his new companion.

"Yes," said Harry, and it was a relief to say it out loud. "I have seen the Gluttonous Beast." He felt as if he had just confessed to a priest. At least he imagined that was what it felt like, having not seen the inside of a church for twenty years.

"And what of him?"

Harry frowned. "Such an ugly creature, put me right off my food, he has."

"Tell me this," said the man. "What is it about the Beast that makes you want to see him?"

"Well," said Harry, walking again. "I can't say what it is exactly. But it's like with all ugliness, you want to look away but you can't."

"Can't?" queried the stranger.

"It's very difficult," said Harry, almost apologetically. "Why do you ask?"

The man seemed not to hear. "Do you think the Beast should be on display?"

"Why not?" replied Harry, by now a little confused and

slightly uneasy. It wasn't often a complete stranger in the City would strike up a conversation. Usually they would say "Give me your money" in a threatening way. Under other circumstances—that is, Harry not being in shock after a difficult experience—he probably would have run away. "What else can someone, some*thing*, like the Gluttonous Beast do?" he said. "Didn't God put such creatures on earth for our amusement? It's a reminder to us all to thank the Lord it ain't us. Poor wretches." For a nonreligious man, Harry seemed unusually preoccupied with God at this moment.

"Do you think this creature wishes to be stared upon?"

Harry was growing tired of this inquisition. "People needs their entertainment, you know. I paid money to see the Beast and that's what I saw. Anyhow, I'm on my way home, so I'll bid you good night."

The man chose that moment to step in front of Harry, blocking his way. Harry, exasperated and a little frightened, turned into the short lane on his right that sloped down to the river. He walked quickly, but he knew the man was following; he could hear footsteps crunching in the icy snow and at the same time a strange high-pitched whirring noise. Harry turned around, his back to the river, and challenged the oncoming stranger.

"Why are you following me?"

"You've told me all I want to know," he said, again ignoring the question, "and I thank you for your time." Then, before Harry knew what was happening, his pursuer thrust a short stick at his portly stomach. Harry felt a sudden shock of pain explode through his body, causing him to leap backward, stunned and breathless, clutching at his chest. He heard the whirring noise again.

"What's—going—on?" he gasped.

"Nothing you'll ever know about," came the reply.

Harry felt another shocking blow and fell onto the wall, his head dangling over the water. He could hear and smell the Foedus below. In one swift movement the man shoved something into Harry's waistcoat pocket and then he felt strong hands gripping him around his ankles and he was lifted over the edge. His last thought was *What's that in my pocket?* for it wasn't a carrot or an onion. Then the water parted like a tear in cheap fabric only to close over him, the gash mended invisibly, and he sank into oblivion.

CHAPTER NINE

Deodonatus Snoad

There was really no way to describe Deodonatus Snoad other than downright ugly. And even to say that would be considered a kindness. His ugliness was unique in its physical manifestation. His stubby neck was lumpy and supported, at an angle, a most unfortunate head that was far too big for his crooked body. On his lopsided face there sat a large red misshapen nose and a pair of muddy eyes that were half hidden under his protruding brow. He was a hairy chap and his eyebrows ran into each other in one long bushy line that dipped slightly to meet on the bridge of his nose. Like many of his fellow citizens, his teeth, at least those that remained, were in pretty poor shape and caused him pain on a daily basis. But Deodonatus had never been one for smiling.

Deodonatus was ugly as a baby, which was not unusual, but even his own mother thought he was a little hard on the eyes. As he grew, people would stare at him in the street and then cross over to avoid him. He quickly realized that the world outside his house was a cruel place so he spent his time indoors, shut away in his room. He had an agile mind and taught himself to read and write and educated himself in all that was considered worthwhile in his day.

As for his parents, perhaps once Deodonatus had loved them, but soon he scorned them. They had always found it difficult to look at him, his mother especially, and with his ever-increasing erudition they soon had little enough to say to him. Shortly after his tenth birthday, they decided they had fulfilled their parental responsibilities (and admirably so, they thought, under the circumstances) and one morning they sold him to a traveling show.

Deodonatus spent the next eight years going from town to town, exhibiting under the imaginative title of "Mr. Hideous." His act consisted of sitting stony-faced on a three-legged stool in a small booth for the sole purpose of being stared at. And how people loved to stare! Occasionally he also had to suffer the indignity of being prodded. Only then would he react with a vicious snarl, which made the women scream and the men utter such phrases as "By Jove, but he's a fiery monster!"

And as Deodonatus sat there and watched the people gape at him and put their hands to their mouths in horror, he considered the nature of mankind and concluded that the whole human race was hateful and deserved every misfortune that fell upon it, either by luck or by design. This was an important distinction. Deodonatus now harbored thoughts of revenge. Not on anyone in particular—that would come later—though perhaps his parents might have crossed his mind as worthy candidates once or twice. Deodonatus had a good grasp of economics and fully endorsed the concept of supply and demand. A man must make a living and the show's owner was only giving the people what they wanted. If any blame was to be apportioned, then it fell on the general public who came to gawk.

Deodonatus performed as Mr. Hideous until his eighteenth year. He grew a thick beard and one night soon after, he slipped away, but not before tying up the proprietor and taking all his money. Thus endowed, he made his way to Urbs Umida, a city renowned for its own ugliness, in the hope that he might be able to merge into the crowds and live a relatively peaceful life.

They say that beauty is in the eye of the beholder, but experience had taught Deodonatus otherwise. He had learned that if he was to hope to have any quality of life, then it was best that he wasn't beheld at all. It is also said that one must not judge a book by its cover. After all, it is a universal truth that what really matters is the substance between the front and the back. In Deodonatus Snoad's case, however, when you looked past his repulsive appearance and laid open his particular book, what was within was much worse than that which was without. Molded by his youthful experiences, Deodonatus was a bitter and twisted man, physically and mentally, almost wholly beyond redemption.

***

The very first time Deodonatus passed through the gates to enter the south side of Urbs Umida, he felt as if he was coming home. He looked around and smiled. Such an ugly and evil city, full of hypocrisy and deceit. He took lodgings in the most insalubrious part of town and soon settled in. He savored the ripe smell of the Foedus in the summer months and he smirked at the homeless wretches in puddles and huddles in the winter. Occasionally he would even venture into the Nimble Finger Inn and stand at the back to observe his fellow citizens at their worst.

He lived well, at first, on his ill-gotten gains, but he knew that eventually he would need an income. But what? He was aware of *The Urbs Umida Daily Chronicle*, a popular newspaper that had a wide readership because of its sensational headlines, simple words, and large fonts. Deodonatus wrote a piece on the state of the pavements (constantly being dug up to repair inefficient water pipes) and had it delivered to the newspaper. It was well received. They liked his outraged tone, his sarcasm, and asked for more, which he duly provided.

And that was the beginning of Deodonatus's career with the *Chronicle*.

Deodonatus worked from the comfort of his lodgings. The landlady, no great beauty herself, considered money a cure for most things, repulsion included, and was happy to give this stranger a large room at the top with a view over the City. Deodonatus required little else and, luckily for all concerned, preferred his own company. So he hid away from the world during the day and rarely ventured out before sundown. He delivered his pieces to the newspaper by means of the landlady's son who, for a penny, came every day to collect them.

At night, after he returned from his regular nocturnal walks, he would sit beside the fire and read. The days of Mr. Hideous seemed very far away and occasionally he was overcome by a strange feeling he couldn't identify. It was, perhaps, the slightest glimmer of happiness.

Deodonatus felt safe now, surrounded by all that was important to him, namely his collection of books, within the pages of which he could be transported from the depressing reality of daily life in the City. In his more contemplative moments he liked to consider the words of the ancient philosophers, both Roman and Greek, for they had plenty to say to a man in his circumstances. Deodonatus also had a particular penchant for fairy tales. It seemed to him that in these stories an inordinate number of characters were rescued from hideousness and turned into beautiful people. But in the harsh light of day, when he uncovered the mirror that he kept to remind him why he was there, his reflection told him that his life was far from a fairy tale.

So he turned down the lamps and kept the mirror covered but left the shutters open to watch and hear the sounds of the City. He made his room comfortable and kept it tidy, except for his desk. It was strewn with a plethora of writing materials, paper, quills and inkpots, and a copy of Jonsen's Dictionary. Pinned to the wall he had some of the pieces that he had recently written, one of which outlined the dangers of speeding horses and carts. He had thought the headline particularly good:

Careening Carts Cause Murderous and Muddy Mayhem

Tonight, while Juno was slumbering in a fog of herbs and Pin was recording his eventful life in his journal, Deodonatus was standing at the window looking out over the white roofs. They glistened in the intermittent moonlight in complete contrast to the Foedus, whose black waters greedily swallowed the light. Deodonatus was restless these days. He paced up and down the room, muttering to himself and fidgeting his hair into knots. After half an hour he went to his desk, dipped his quill in the ink, and began to write feverishly.

CHAPTER TEN

Article from

𝕿𝖍𝖊 𝖀𝖗𝖇𝖘 𝖀𝖒𝖎𝖉𝖆 𝕯𝖆𝖎𝖑𝖞 𝕮𝖍𝖗𝖔𝖓𝖎𝖈𝖑𝖊

BEASTLY GOINGS-ON AT THE NIMBLE FINGER
BY
DEODONATUS SNOAD

My Dear Readers,

I am sure that by now there are very few of you out there who have not seen, or at the very least heard of, the latest goings-on in the Nimble Finger, that inn of ill repute—well earned, I might say—on the Bridge. If nothing else one must commend the landlady, Betty Peggotty, for her business sense. Who could forget the mermaid she had on show just a few weeks ago? Granted her tail was a little limp and perhaps she was not as pleasing to the eye as one would imagine such a divine aquatic creature to be—she seemed quite advanced in years; perhaps that is how she was caught in the first place—nevertheless, she was for all intents and purposes a living, breathing, occasionally gasping, mermaid.

Prior to that, if I recall correctly, Mrs. Peggotty

had on show a centaur by the name of Mr. Ephcott. Although I never spoke to the fellow, I heard that he was surprisingly well read and displayed exquisite manners. A little stiff-legged, particularly in his hind legs, but certainly a most pleasing entertainment. And that, after all, is what we poor citizens of Urbs Umida are looking for, is it not?

Mermaids, centaurs, and other such exotic creatures aside, I must say I think the good Mrs. Peggotty has now surpassed herself. Not only does she have the place full from morning to night with drunken hordes (some would consider them entertainment enough!) filling her coffers, but of late she has a wild creature of another kind altogether in her cellar—namely the Gluttonous Beast. The place is a veritable circus!

My duty as always is to you, Dear Readers. So with this in mind I went to see for myself this Gluttonous Beast. And I can confirm that everything I have heard is true. He is an horrendous creature of indeterminate species and insatiable appetite. It is deemed imperative that he be contained behind bars. His temper is unpredictable and he feeds on raw meat of the foulest kind, though he has a particular taste for Jocastar, that sheeplike animal so prized for its wool. There is nothing like a beast with expensive taste, I say. He is not alone in this city!

Beasts aside, I must move on, although it pains

me, to other, graver, matters. It is with great regret and heartache I report that the Silver Apple Killer has struck again. Another body, the fourth, was dragged from the Foedus early this morning. None of us has yet forgotten the matter of Oscar Carpue and the murder of Fabian Merdegrave. Mr. Carpue, to my mind certainly the most likely culprit, has yet to be found. Many think that he has fled the City to evade the gallows. But I am not of that opinion. What, I wonder, could he tell us of the Silver Apple Killer? After all, birds of similar plumage fly as one. It is hardly beyond reason to think that the two, the Silver Apple Killer and Oscar Carpue, might in fact be one. Granted no apple was found in Fabian's pocket, but who knows the workings of a murderer's mind?

Think on it, Dear Readers, and you are bound to agree!

Until next time,

Deodonatus Snoad

Deodonatus signed off with a satisfied flourish, rolled up the paper, and tied it with string. Evil was everywhere. It was in human nature. As was the love of power, a power Deodonatus wielded with his written word. What pleasure it gave him to wander the streets at night to hear the people talking about what he had written!

Deodonatus had an avid following among the readers of

the *Chronicle*. There were daily meetings in the coffeehouses and taverns and gatherings on street corners just to hear what Deodonatus had to say on the latest issues in the City. They didn't always understand what he wrote, but they believed it (for if it was printed in the *Chronicle* it had to be true) and they were proud to be called "Dear Readers." It made them feel as if someone out there actually cared and that was as much as was required to have their lifelong loyalty. Conversely, Deodonatus held his audience in contempt.

Impatiently he pulled a handle that hung from the ceiling just by the door, and from somewhere in the house came the muffled tinkling of a bell. A minute later there was the sound of light footsteps up the stairs and then a knock at the door. Deodonatus opened it a couple of inches.

"Have you got something for me, Mr. Snoad?" This was followed by a yawn—the hour was late.

Deodonatus handed the cylinder of paper through the crack.

"Out by tomorrow, eh?" said the boy. "We're all looking forward to reading it."

"Huh," grunted Deodonatus. And shut the door.

CHAPTER ELEVEN

Home Sweet Home

Pin knelt on the floor and carefully poured some water into the coconut shells he had placed under each leg of his bed. It was the best way he knew to stop bugs and lice from crawling into his mattress. As soon as he thought of "bugs," he was immediately reminded of Deodonatus Snoad. He had seen his latest piece in the *Chronicle*.

That sleazy cockroach, thought Pin venomously. *How dare he! Suggesting* again *that my father might be the Silver Apple Killer.*

Wasn't it enough that in the weeks after Fabian Merdegrave was throttled, Deodonatus had written daily about Oscar Carpue's supposed part in his death? And every day he slandered him and accused him of murder. *Without a potato peeling of evidence*, thought Pin. *Absence is hardly the same as guilt.* He clenched his fists and ground his teeth. Deodonatus cared little for the truth. *The man is lower than a sludge beetle. If I ever meet him I'll . . . I'll . . .* It was a sentence he finished variously but usually it involved violence.

Pin lay back on his bed with a sigh of exhaustion. He

didn't lie for long. The mattress felt no more than a straw or two thick and the boards beneath were as hard as rock. Barton Gumbroot was not the sort of landlord who ever considered his lodgers' comfort. As far as he was concerned, Pin should think it a bonus to have a bed at all; most rooms had just a mattress on the floor.

Even now, days after his strange experience in the *Cella Moribundi*, Pin couldn't get it out of his head—or his nose. The aroma of the artemisia and myrrh lingered in his shirt, a constant reminder to him of that eerie night.

Although he could not show it, Mr. Gaufridus was a sensitive man in his own way and, when he saw Pin the morning after his experience with poor Sybil, he knew immediately that something had happened. Pin seemed decidedly distracted, toe pulling and sole pricking well beyond the call of duty. Regardless of Pin's dedication to his work, the broken door lock and muddy footprints in the *Cella Moribundi* also testified to the presence of rather more than one boy and a dead body.

"Is there something you want to tell me?" asked Mr. Gaufridus.

Pin was not the ablest of dissemblers. Under Mr. Gaufridus's icy gaze he told him everything and it was a relief to let it out.

"It was all like a dream," finished Pin. "I'm not sure it happened at all, and of course I was drugged. I am convinced that I have been the victim of some cunning illusionist. For what I saw is simply not possible."

Mr. Gaufridus, also a practical soul, was of the same opinion. He was not wholly unsympathetic to Pin's plight—after all, the boy had been rendered senseless—and there was certainly little evidence that Sybil had enjoyed a brief respite from her eternal rest. Sybil herself was taken away to the churchyard later that morning and as Mr. Gaufridus closed the door in her wake, Pin hung his head, gripping the soles of his tatty boots with his toes.

"I should have heard them, I should have stopped them," he said miserably. "Do you still wish me to work here?"

Mr. Gaufridus harrumphed loudly. He would have smiled if he could. He liked the boy. Pin worked hard. He could not be blamed for what had happened. Yes, he might threaten that there were plenty of others out there on the streets who would pull toes for a living, but he had to admit that he was doubtful about their actual number. He was also certain he would not find anyone as honest and conscientious as Pin. As for whether his father was a murderer or not, unlike many Urbs Umidians, Mr. Gaufridus was rather ahead of his time in the respect that he felt guilt should be proven, not assumed.

"Yes," he said kindly, though he couldn't help adding sternly for measure, "but don't let this happen again."

So Pin sat on the edge of his bed and tried not to think any more about Sybil or Deodonatus Snoad. Footsteps sounded on the wooden stairs outside. He recognized that heavy tread and groaned. Barton Gumbroot might be light-fingered, but he certainly wasn't light-footed.

He waited for the inevitable slapping sound. Barton always used the flat of his hand and not his knuckles when he knocked. Pin went to the door and his lip curled. Barton's peculiar odor signified his presence even through the wooden door. He smelled of many things, but overwhelmingly of dried blood (someone else's) and bad breath (his own).

Barton Gumbroot stood outside in the gloomy corridor in his usual attire: a gray shirt (perhaps it had once been white) with wide sleeves pulled in by strings at the cuff, a suspiciously stained waistcoat, and a dark pair of cloth breeches of indeterminate origin. His neckerchief was stiff with dried food and his boots were spattered with mud and other matter that did not require closer examination.

But it wasn't Barton's clothes that concerned Pin. It was the shifty look on his face. Pin knew it meant one of two things. He was either going to ask for more money (as he had done three times already in the recent past) or he was going to ask him to leave.

"I've got some news for you, lad," Gumbroot began, rubbing his knuckles with the palm of his hand, the dry skin rasping softly.

Pin folded his arms across his chest and stood with his feet wide apart. He had found it was the best way to deal with the man. He looked him up and down, his face expressionless.

"What is it?"

"Rent's going up."

"But you know I cannot pay any more than I do," protested Pin.

Barton stared shamelessly at Pin's mouth. "There's always another way," he suggested slyly.

Pin's eyes widened and he half-shouted, "No!" Barton shrugged. He looked around the door and sized up the room. "I could have four times as many people in here."

"You mean four people."

Gumbroot looked confused. He wasn't one for mathematics. He sniffed. He was always slightly nervous at evictions. This was not out of any concern for those he was about to throw out, but more because he feared the ructions it would cause. To be evicted from Barton Gumbroot's lodgings was usually the last straw for desperate people, and desperate people do desperate things.

"Don't play clever with me, young lad. I need you out by the morning."

"I don't suppose I have any choice," said Pin bitterly.

Gumbroot pulled at his nose with finger and thumb and cocked his head to one side. "That's about the long and short of it," he said with some satisfaction. "I knew you'd understand. You always were an intelligent—"

That was when Pin shut the door.

"In fact, if you could do me the favor of leaving *tonight*," came Mr. Gumbroot's disembodied voice from the other side, "I'd be much obliged."

And so later that evening Pin left. He knew if he didn't go, the next time he came back he'd find his belongings on the street and a whole new family moved in. That's how it was around here. He packed his bag with what little he had and took off.

"I suppose at least now I might find something better," he had reasoned, trying to stay cheerful. And at least he no longer had to listen to the screams coming from the basement. There had certainly been something unspeakable going on down there tonight. But for all his optimism Pin was worried. Winter was never a good time to be looking for rooms in Urbs Umida and tonight most likely he would be on the street.

CHAPTER TWELVE

An Evening's Entertainment

MRS. BETTY PEGGOTTY (Proprietor) Is Pleased To Announce A New Arrival At

THE NIMBLE FINGER INN

For your *DELIGHT* and *DELECTATION*

The BONE MAGICIAN

See Him Breathe Life Into
DEAD BONES DAILY | ENTRY **SIXPENCE**
YOU WILL NOT BE DISAPPOINTED

ALSO SEE THE

GLUTTONOUS BEAST

A TRULY HORRIFIC CREATURE OF INSATIABLE APPETITE

ENTRY SIXPENCE | REFRESHMENTS AVAILABLE ALL DAY IN THE INN | **OPEN EARLY UNTIL LATE**

From where he was standing sheltered by the doorway of the Nimble Finger, Pin could easily read the discarded handbill that lay at his feet, one of many that littered the gutters.

The Gluttonous Beast. Deodonatus Snoad—Pin spat at the mere mention of his name—had written of him recently. And the Bone Magician . . . That could be interesting. Pin had a few pennies in his pocket—he had left Barton's owing rent—but did he want to spend them here? The decision was made for him when a large shadow fell over him. It was Constable Coggley.

"And what might you be up to? You can't hang about 'ere, you know." He peered at Pin curiously. "Do I know you?"

"I don't think so," said Pin, shrinking back.

"But I do," said Coggley, taking him by the chin and forcing his head upward. "You're that Pin Carpue. You can't deny your queer eyes. What you up to now, lad. Causing trouble?"

"No," said Pin indignantly, jerking his face away. He pushed against the heavy inn door and it yielded slowly.

"Have you seen your father?" called Coggley after him. "You'd better tell me if you have. He's still a wanted man."

"I know," muttered Pin, "I know," and he stepped inside.

The Nimble Finger Inn was one of many taverns that had occupied the same spot on the Bridge for centuries. It was a good spot, exactly at the halfway point, which meant people could feel that they hadn't crossed to the other side. For if the northerners were reluctant to venture south, the southerners had no great desire to venture north. Whatever its name and whoever its owner, one thing hadn't changed down the years: the quality of the clientele. It was often said that if you were a visitor to Urbs Umida, all you had to do was step inside the Nimble Finger to see a true representation of everything the City had to offer. It was all in there: the dirt, the smell, and the good citizens themselves; the robbers, the swindlers, the cheats, the liars, the fakes, and the forgers. Northerners and southerners alike and all treated equally by Betty Peggotty. Well, as equally as their purses allowed.

The floor was covered with a mixture of sawdust and straw and mud and stains of a sanguinary nature. The noise was deafening—singing, shouting, screeching, laughter. And the smells. Oh, those smells. To Pin they were like a riotous odoriferous cacophony and he breathed deeply. All the excitement of the inn came to him on the air and he savored it. There was gambling going on, he could smell the tension; there was plotting afoot, he could smell the fear; and there was jollity and excitement. He smelt it all: the blood, the sweat, the salty tears, the drink, the fish from the dockworkers, and always the exotic aroma of faraway lands from the sailors. There was even a hint of love—only a hint, mind you; the Nimble Finger was not really a courting sort of place. Having inhaled his fill, he turned to the man next to him.

"The Bone Magician?" he asked. A grunt and a gnarled finger pointed him in the direction of the far side of the tavern, where he could see a set of stairs. A man stood at the top outside an open door. Pin ascended, his curiosity awakening.

"That'll be sixpence," said the fellow at the door. "And you can ask a question."

"Whom shall I ask?"

"Madame de Bona."

"Oh," said Pin. He could see into the room and it was already full of people.

"Well, hand it over, then," said the fellow impatiently. "They shuts the door at eight."

Pin found himself standing at the back of a crowd in the darkened room. Feet were shuffling and muttered conversations were going on all around him and snatches came to his alert ears.

"I 'eard as she tells the future like, this Bona woman."

"I suppose she can see it, being as she's passed over 'n' that."

"'Ere, listen to this, God strike me down if I tell a lie, but Molly, you know 'er what lives opposite, well, she asked about 'er poor Fred, you know, what fell in the Foedus the other day."

"Pushed, weren't 'e? Some finks she did it."

"Wotever. But she says to 'er, the Bona skelington, that 'e was 'appy and waiting for 'er. And don't you know, she died the next day and went to join 'im."

"Never! In the Foedus?"

"Wot? Nah, not in the river, in the grave."

"Wotever, there's plenty in the Foedus these days, with that fruit killer around."

Pin squeezed through the crowd to the front where he could see a raised platform. On a low table a foot or so from the edge there was a shallow coffin. It was roughly hewn, with a badly fitting lid, and Pin thought of Mr. Gaufridus with a smile. It wasn't up to his exacting standards. At the back of the platform was a four-paneled screen and Pin could see movement behind it.

Suddenly the crowd quietened. A man dressed from head to toe in a black gown stepped out from behind the screen. A silver brooch at his throat pinned in place a dark velvet cloak that fell in folds from his shoulders. The heavy material, beautifully decorated with vines and fruit stitched in amber and gold, flapped around his ankles as he walked to reveal its shimmering scarlet lining. His shoes, visible under the hem of his gown, were also of a gold fabric with a slight heel and tasseled toes that pointed upward. With each step he took, the tassels rustled quietly.

His face was concealed in the main by a large hood that fell over his forehead, shielding his eyes. His eyebrows were thick and gray and his pale skin glowed unnaturally. He wore a moustache on his upper lip, each end waxed and carefully arranged on either side of his mouth, and a narrow white beard sprouted from the tip of his chin. His sleeves were so long that when his hands hung at his sides, his fingernails were barely visible and his slender wrists were seen only when he stretched out his arms.

Then a second person came around the screen, also hooded and cloaked, in a dark cloth of plain weave, its only ornament being the gold toggles that fastened it. The figure stepped gracefully from the platform and began walking slowly through the audience, swinging a peardrop bottle on a silver chain rhythmically back and forth. A smoky mist of sweet perfume curled upward in a lazy spiral from its slender neck. Pin's heart began to race and his knees began to shake. He knew that smell.

"Welcome, all," said the man finally. "My name is Benedict Pantagus and I am the Bone Magician."

CHAPTER THIRTEEN

Pin's Journal

I sit at this very moment in a dark corner in the Nimble Finger. I have pennies enough for a small ale and I have secured an uneven table whereupon I am endeavoring to write an account of the night's entertainment. What a city of trickery this is! Only days ago I thought I had seen the strangest it could offer. I had not considered there could be more. And now, such a night I've had in the Nimble Finger, confronted once more by the people who drugged me and left me insensible in the Cella Moribundi. Can you imagine how I felt when I realized who they were? I should have been riven with fury, but instead, with every inhalation of the aromas in the room, I was suffused with peace and calm to bear witness again, upright and awake this time, to a most intriguing performance. And this is what I saw.

Mr. Pantagus, after his introduction, returned to the head of the coffin.

"My good people," he said, "a Bone Magician is born, not made.

I have inherited my skills with the dead from a long line of Bone Magicians. I from my father, and he from his, and he from his. And so it goes on through the centuries right back to ancient times. The world might be a different place today, with the advance of philosophies and sciences, but be assured, there is still room in this day and age for those of us who can bring the dead back to life."

At this there was a ripple of assenting murmurs. Mr. Pantagus gestured toward the coffin.

"I am a privileged man. I have been charged with the care of this coffin within which lies the skeleton of one Madame Celestine de Bona. I ask now that you remain silent while I perform the ceremony that will bring about her revitalization."

Juno, whom I now knew the second figure to be, quenched the candles around the walls, leaving for light only the four thick beeswax pillars on tall iron holders, one at each corner of the platform. Mr. Pantagus removed the lid of the coffin and laid it aside. Then, by means of a series of internal latches, he dropped each side of the coffin to rest flat on the table, exposing the box's grisly contents.

A hush descended on the room and we all leaned forward as one, our curiosity stronger than our fear, to see more clearly what it was before us. For there, in full view of this awestruck crowd, lay the arid brown bones of Madame de Bona.

I watched, awash in a confusion of emotions, openmouthed in amazement, as Benedict Pantagus began a series of actions that I recognized immediately as identical to those I had witnessed so recently in the Cella

Moribundi. And I smelled again cinnamon and myrrh, anise and artemisia, as I waited with mounting excitement for the inevitable.

The skeleton began to stir.

A shudder went through the fleshless frame from skull to toe, rattling its bones. Its jaw hung open slightly and its grinning mouth emitted a whining groan, the like of which I had only imagined in my nightmares but had never thought to hear. The crowd gasped and shrank away from the vile unearthly creature before them. There was a shrill cry at the back of the room and a young lady collapsed. Such was the entrancement of the people that she was left to come to on her own on the floor.

If, as Mr. Pantagus claimed, the skeleton had been a lady, little remained to indicate this except perhaps to the eye of an expert. She rose slowly, like a ship on the swell of a wave, and came forward until she was sitting bolt upright. She placed her hands on the coffin sides for support, her long bony fingers clicking on the wood. Finally she opened her surprisingly toothy jaws fully in what appeared to be a yawn.

Mr. Pantagus had our full attention as his deep and sonorous voice resonated in the tense atmosphere.

"Ladies and gentlemen, may I present to you the revitalized bones of Madame Celestine de Bona."

We took this as our cue to applaud, doing so loudly and with an unfettered enthusiasm. Mr. Pantagus's beard twitched and I believe he smiled briefly.

"My thanks," he said graciously and he gave a shallow bow. "Now let us move quickly on to our real purpose. Madame de Bona, alive and well as she appears, will not be with us for long. As you are aware, your sixpence allows one question. Perhaps you wish to know the fate of a loved one who has also passed over to the other side. Or maybe you have a question about yourself. Whatever the problem, Madame de Bona will attempt to provide the answer."

The people murmured to one another, too nervous to speak directly to this strange Bone Magician and his skeleton friend.

"Surely you are not shy?" he asked, almost playfully. "Please, consider the feelings of Madame de Bona. When she was alive she was one of the world's greatest soothsayers. Do not deny her the pleasure of doing the same from beyond the grave."

His entreaty seemed to work and a young man shuffled forward. His cheeks were flushed. "Is it true that she, Madame de Bona, can foretell the future?"

"A revitalized body is blessed with foresight, indeed," replied Mr. Pantagus. "Have you a question for her?"

"Tell me, Madame de Bona," he said nervously, "will I ever fall in love?"

The silence was so thick it could have been split in two with an axe. Madame de Bona cocked her head to one side and it was easy to imagine that if there had been eyeballs in those sockets, they would have been rolled toward heaven in contemplation. She leaned ever so slightly in the young man's direction and replied in a voice that surely came only from the underworld, "Yes."

This single word excited the crowd greatly. I cannot deny that I too was quite moved, and the lad was pulled back roughly before he had a chance to say another word (I would have asked "when?") by a large rotund man who went right up to the platform and put out his hand.

"Madame," he began breathlessly, but before he could continue, Mr. Pantagus frowned. "Madame de Bona does not wish to be touched," he said sternly.

The man flushed and stepped back immediately, apologizing.

"Tell me, Madame, why won't my chickens lay?"

Madame de Bona fixed her empty sockets on the man and replied scornfully, "I do not answer questions about chickens."

The man looked beseechingly at Mr. Pantagus, but he only shrugged sympathetically.

After that, there followed a plethora of questions about a multitude of topics, generally the everyday concerns of citizens in a place such as Urbs Umida. There was laughter at her replies, gasps, nods, and shakes of the head. By the end the atmosphere was as jolly as the tavern downstairs. Eventually Mr. Pantagus held up his hand and the noise quieted and we stood hanging on his every word.

"Just one more question," said Mr. Pantagus finally. "Time is running out. Madame de Bona will soon be exhausted."

I thought it was Mr. Pantagus who sounded exhausted. His voice, deep and throaty earlier, was strained. Before I could help it, I heard myself say, "I have a question."

All eyes were on me and they lingered as usual, knowing that there was something different about my face, but not quite sure what.

"Madame de Bona," I said carefully, "where is my father and why did he disappear?"

"That's two questions," muttered the man with the reluctant chickens.

Madame de Bona took her time answering. The crowd was beginning to shuffle its feet. "Carpue boy," I heard someone say from behind and I felt my cheeks flush bright red, but I maintained a steady gaze at Madame de Bona.

"Child," came the soft reply, "your father is alive and not as far away as you think. Keep searching and you will find the truth."

I was shaking. I wanted them to stop looking at me and whispering. At last, Mr. Pantagus spoke.

"My dear ladies and gentlemen," he said quickly, "there will be no more questions this evening. I should like to thank you all for coming to see us and we hope you will tell all your friends about us."

As if on cue, the skeleton sank slowly back down into the coffin, her bones giving one final rattle when her skull touched the wood. The crowd cheered and clapped loudly. The door behind them was opened and they shuffled out of the fragrant room into the not-so-fragrant tavern.

I watched Mr. Pantagus and Juno swiftly put the coffin together again. Then my view was blocked by people stepping onto the platform and examining the coffin. Out of curiosity I too went to look, but it was empty and there was no sign of the Bone Magician or the girl. I looked around the screen and saw a door in the wall. I tried the handle, the door opened on to a staircase, and I descended to another door at the bottom. I stepped out into the alley that ran down the side of the Nimble Finger. The Foedus was to my left, to my right the thoroughfare over the Bridge.

The alley was empty. In the fresh cold air I pondered what I had just seen and the answer I had been given. I could feel a resurgence of hope in my heart. Perhaps my father was still in the City after all. But with the hope came anxiety. If I did see him again, then I would find out the truth. But was that what I really wanted?

CHAPTER FOURTEEN

A Chance Encounter

Out on the street Pin took his hat from his pocket and pulled it down over his ears, then raised the collar of his coat to meet it. Unfortunately there was a deficit of material in the middle, leaving the back of his head exposed. The cold gripped his skull like a vice. The warmth of the ale and the inn were long gone.

I cannot stay out in this tonight, he thought. *I shall be dead before morning.*

Pin could not recall a winter this cold. Even the Foedus looked more sluggish than usual. He knew he had to keep moving. He set off, not knowing where he was going, but stumbled almost immediately on something hard underfoot. A potato. He hoped that it might be hot. This was not as unrealistic as it might sound. Many people carried hot potatoes in their pockets for warmth and, of course, ultimately to eat. But this was not cooked. It still had the earth clinging to it. And it was a most peculiar shape, greatly swollen at one end, tapering almost to a point at the other. Except for its dark red skin, Pin might have thought it was a carrot.

"I'll be having that if you don't mind."

Pin looked around at the sound of the voice, but he could see no one.

"Pardon?" he said. Then he felt a tap on his lower back and looked down to see a short, in fact a very short, solid-bodied man looking up at him.

"Oh," said Pin, for want of anything better to say, and handed over the potato.

The man took it and slipped it in his pocket. "Many thanks," he said, and he held out his right hand—in his left he had a pipe—and introduced himself, taking Pin's hand with a firm grip. His palm felt rough and muddy.

"Beag Hickory," he said pleasantly, looking Pin right in the eye albeit with his head cocked back at an acute angle. "Pleased to make your acquaintance."

"B-yug," repeated Pin. "How would you spell that?"

"B-E-A-G. It means 'small.'"

Pin started to laugh, but when he saw Beag's arch-browed expression he stopped.

"It makes sense," said Pin, listening carefully. Beag had a rather pronounced accent, with rolling r's; most definitely he was not a native of the City. "After all, you are—"

"A dwarf," cut in Beag. "I am that, but for sure haven't we all our crosses to bear in this life. Some easier, of course, than others." He looked at Pin, waiting patiently.

"Oh," said Pin, suddenly realizing what he wanted. "My name is Pin."

"Just Pin?"

"Pin Carpue," said Pin before thinking and then frowned, but Beag said nothing. Perhaps he didn't know about the disgraced Carpue family.

"It's short for Crispin."

"Crispin, eh?" Beag mulled over the name and looked Pin up and down. "Interesting," was all he said. Then, nodding in the direction of the Nimble Finger, "Have you been in, then?"

"I have," replied Pin. "To see the Bone Magician."

"Ah, yes, Mr. Pantagus," said Beag. "A strange trade in my book, though some would say mine is no stranger. And what of the Gluttonous Beast?"

Pin shook his head. "Not yet."

Beag rubbed his hands together and the sound was like sandpaper. He looked at Pin quizzically. "I should think you'll be off home and out of this cold? Never known a winter like it. 'Tis uncommon without a doubt."

"I would be off home," said Pin, rather more pathetically than he intended, "but I lost my room tonight. I suppose I shall be on the street."

"In this city you won't be the only one," remarked Beag drily. "I'm waiting on a friend myself, or I'd be well gone. Should be here any minute—"

"Hold up, my good man," called a voice from behind, and then there was the sound of running footsteps.

Pin wondered whom Beag might know who spoke in such a way, distinctly northern, and he waited with interest to see who this fellow was. The man who came up to them was tall, significantly so, and his slim frame was accentuated by the long dark coat he wore, which was fastened up to the neck. Pin thought he looked most elegant and strikingly handsome.

"Glad I caught up with you," he said, clapping Beag heartily on the back. "I don't fancy being out on my own these nights. Might get thrown into the Foedus by that madman, what is it they call him? The Silver Apple Killer."

"That's what Deodonatus Snoad calls him," said Beag.

"And who is this young fellow?" asked the man, as if suddenly realizing that the scruffy boy beside Beag might actually be with him. "Aren't you going to introduce me?"

"Pin," said Beag, "allow me to present my great friend, Mr. Aluph Buncombe."

"Pleased to meet you," said Pin politely and touched his hat.

"What exquisite manners," said Mr. Buncombe with a quick smile, looking him up and down. "Surely not learned this side of the river?"

"'Twas my mother," said Pin. "She was from over the river too. She taught me that manners cost little but are worth a lot."

"A sensible woman," replied Aluph, rather pleased that Pin should take him for a northerner. He had spent many hours perfecting his vowels.

"She was," said Pin quietly.

"Pin has lost his lodgings," said Beag. "I wondered if Mrs. Hoadswood might be able to help out."

"Well," said Aluph confidently. "If there was ever a woman who would try her best to fix you up, it's Mrs. Hoadswood. Certainly at the very least she'll give you a dinner."

Pin's eyes lit up at the prospect.

"I can't promise anything else," warned Beag.

Aluph was blowing on his gloved hands, impatient to go, so the three of them set off.

"Tell me, young man," asked Aluph conversationally, "how did the two of you come upon each other?"

"I tripped over Mr. Hickory's potato."

Aluph laughed. "You're lucky it didn't hit you in the head."

Pin looked confused and Aluph glanced at Beag. "Have you not told him?"

"Told me what?" asked Pin.

Aluph didn't give Beag time to speak. "Why, of his great talents. Beag here may be small in stature, but he is an intellectual giant."

Beag smiled and took a bow. "Mr. Buncombe, sir, you are too kind."

"What are your talents?" asked Pin, still wondering where the potato came into it.

Beag puffed up with pride and spoke as if to a rather larger audience than he actually had.

"I, Beag Hickory, am a son of faraway lands, a poet and bard, a scholar—"

"Oh, we know all that," interrupted Aluph. "Tell him what you really do."

Beag looked a little crestfallen, cut off as he was in full flow, but he obliged. "I am a poet, that is true, but Urbs Umidians do not appreciate talents such as that, so I have taken a different course in life. Though it is hardly the future I was promised when I sat on the *Cathaoir Feasa.*"

"The *cathaoir* what?" asked Pin.

"Forget that," said Aluph impatiently. "Tell him what it is you do."

"I," said Beag, "am a potato thrower."

For the second time that evening Pin held back his laughter. Beag looked up and down the road and pointed in the distance.

"See that post down there?"

Pin looked. There was indeed a lamppost farther down the street.

Beag drew a line in the snow and took three paces back. He took the potato from his pocket and brushed away the loose earth. He grasped it by the convenient handle, ran to the line, and threw it with a loud expulsion of breath. Pin watched as it flew through the air in a long low arc and hit the post with quite a crack.

"Not bad for a poet," said Beag with more than a little pride, and dusted off his hands.

"I suppose, really, you're a *poet*ato thrower," ventured Pin with a grin.

Beag shook his head and laughed quietly.

"He only uses the best, you know," said Aluph helpfully, with the merest hint of a smile. "Hickory Reds."

CHAPTER FIFTEEN

Beag Hickory

Whether or not Hickory Reds were the preferred choice of a potato thrower, it was certainly true that when it came to projecting medium-sized weighty objects through the air, there was no one to match Beag. It wasn't just the distance, you understand; it was also the accuracy with which he threw them.

Beag was a man with many talents and he had left his home village at a young age to see the world, to learn, and to seek his fortune. He was not going to let his lack of stature be an obstacle and by the ripe old age of twenty-four he had achieved two out of three of his fine objectives. He had certainly traveled extensively and had written songs and poems to prove it. Aluph was not wrong in saying he was an intellectual giant. Beag had acquired knowledge that few Urbs Umidians would believe, let alone remember, and he had forgotten more than most could even know. But on the third, the matter of his fortune, Beag had been well and truly thwarted. Of all the facts he had learned, the hardest had to be that there was no money to be made from poetry and singing. But perhaps there was a living to be earned from potato throwing. Certainly it was a talent that appealed to the stunted imaginations of the Urbs Umidians.

Beag had come to the City two winters ago carrying little more than the clothes on his back, the shoes on his feet, and an old leather bag with a wide strap that he wore across his chest. It contained, among other things, his writings: poetry and ballads—in the main lovelorn and unceasingly depressing—that he liked to recite and sing and for which he hoped one day to win acclaim.

He arrived at the city walls late at night and walked around them until he came to one of the four pairs of guarded entrance gates. Unfortunately for Beag, it was the North Gate which led, naturally, into the northern half of the City. As soon as the guards saw his shabby dress and his wet woolen hat and heard his foreign accent, they determined that he should not enter. The pair of them took a step forward in a most aggressive and unfriendly manner and crossed their muskets to block his way. Of course, on account of Beag's size, the muskets crossed in front of his face, which was not the guards' intention, so they lowered them and stood rather awkwardly bent over and challenged him to explain himself.

"My name is Beag Hickory," he said proudly, "and I have come to your fine city to make my fortune." He could not understand why this pronouncement caused such hilarity between the guards.

"Oho," said the uglier of the two, "and how do you intend to do that?"

Beag drew himself up to his full height by means of rising slyly onto the balls of his feet and pulling a peak in his sodden hat (which sagged almost immediately). "I am a poet, a scholar, an entertainer, a teller o' tales—"

"Then you're at the wrong gate," interrupted the other guard sullenly.

"Is this not Urbs Umida?" asked Beag.

"Aye, it is. But you're still at the wrong gate. I suggest you try south of the river," said the first guard, not bothering to stifle a yawn. "You'll find more of your sort down there, or should I say, your *short*." Both men laughed heartily at this witticism.

Beag frowned. "What do you mean, my *sort*?"

"Paupers, chancers, circus acts," replied the guard, and his voice had hardened.

"Try the Nimble Finger Inn on the Bridge," said the other. "Betty Peggotty, the landlady, sometimes she exhibits strange creatures." This set the other guard off into such a paroxysm of laughter that he was rendered incapable of speech.

Beag, who had learned both when to persist and when to yield, rightly concluded that this was one of those times when a person yielded. "Very well," he said, and he withdrew with his dignity intact and a slight gunpowder stain on his waistcoat where the guard had poked him. "You say the Nimble Finger? Perhaps I shall see you again. I bid you good night and good fortune."

And so, some time later, Beag made his entrance rather less grandly than he had hoped through the South Gate. The guards there waved him on without a second glance. Beag could not fail to notice almost immediately that the aroma on the south of the Foedus was distinctly unpleasant and by careful elimination he soon realized that it was due to the river. Yes, the streets were sludgy and muddy and scattered about with all sorts of debris, recognizable as vegetable and animal remains, but it was the river that gave off the odor that made his nose wrinkle involuntarily. Beag walked alongside the Foedus, logically assuming that the bridge he sought must be on it somewhere, until he came to the marketplace. The stallholders were packing up for the day, but there were still plenty of people milling around looking for cheap scraps, so Beag took out from his bag a piece of wood, cleverly hinged to create a small podium, upon which he stood.

"Good evening, my fair ladies and gentlemen," he began. This generous assessment of the gathered company elicited more than a laugh or two but also drew their attention. "Allow me to present myself to you. My name is Beag Hickory and I should like to entertain you with a song."

He began to sing in a mournful, though undoubtedly tuneful, tone, but he had hardly reached the first chorus (one of many) when he heard a strange whistling sound. His eyes being closed he had not anticipated the missile, and received a rotten cabbage on the side of his head.

He opened his eyes to see a second vegetable winging its way toward him, and this time he ducked. The poor fellow behind him took it full in the face. Through all of this Beag continued to sing bravely, or foolishly. Perhaps both.

"Give it a rest," shouted someone and then he was hit again.

"But," spluttered Beag with righteous indignation through a mouthful of tomato, "I have only just begun."

"No, you ain't," called out a small boy at the back. "You're finished," and he and his friends threw a hail of rotten apples.

Beag was infuriated. Never in his life had he experienced such a hostile reception to his endeavors. "You little imp," he shouted at the small boy. He jumped down from the podium, picked up the first thing that came to hand, a large putrid potato, and he threw it with such force and accuracy that when it hit the boy, it knocked him clean off his feet.

"'Ey! That's my son. Wotcher think yer doing?"

Beag stood rooted to the spot at the sight of the largest man he had ever seen. This great ape towered over the crowd and was bearing down on Beag, who was actually shaking in his boots.

By the holy! thought Beag, instantly regaining movement in his legs. He spun on his heel and took off like a streak of lightning. The man and a small baying crowd were still following when he reached the Bridge. He ran onto its cobbled thoroughfare, looking around desperately for somewhere to hide.

"Down here," hissed a voice. "Quick!"

Beag turned sharply and saw a long finger beckoning to him from the corner of an alley, and without a second thought he ran toward it.

"This way," said the tall man whose finger it was, and he pushed open a door in the wall and dragged Beag in just as the crowd reached the entrance to the alley. Beag followed his rescuer up a short flight of stairs and down again into a crowded, low-ceilinged room filled with smoke and laughter.

"Where are we?" asked Beag of his nameless companion.

"The Nimble Finger Inn," said the man. "I don't know about you, but I fancy a jug of ale."

Only minutes later, safely ensconced in a dark corner, Beag and his newfound friend were supping ale from a large jug that had been brought over by the serving maid. Beag was just about to speak when a commotion near the door made his heart pound again. It was the ape man.

"I'm looking for a dwarf," he said and the whole tavern fell silent. A fierce-looking woman—the redoubtable Betty Peggotty—glared at him with her hands on her hips. She wore upon her head an exotic hat that had seen far better days.

"There's no dwarf here, Samuel," she said firmly. "So either have a jug or be off with you."

"Bah," exclaimed the ape but, faced with such a choice, opted without question for the ale, and soon he was as merry as the rest of them.

Beag relaxed and turned to his companion. "Might I ask who you are?"

"My name is Aluph Buncombe."

"Well, Mr. Buncombe, I owe you my life," said Beag and he shook his hand gratefully.

"Think nothing of it," said Aluph with a broad smile. "Always ready to help a fellow in trouble, though I can't imagine how you had such a man as Samuel Lenacre after you."

Beag explained his sorry tale and Aluph listened with sympathy.

"You're looking for work, you say. What skills have you? Do you tumble?"

Beag laughed and shook his head wryly. "I can, of course. Is there a dwarf out there these days who cannot? But I think perhaps you will favor my other talents."

Aluph raised an eyebrow. "And these are?"

"I am a poet and a balladeer."

Aluph wrinkled his brow worriedly. "I am sure you are, but if you wish to earn money enough to survive in a city such as this, then you must know your audience. Look around you, my friend, and tell me, do these people want stories or poetry?"

Beag surveyed the room and felt despair settling in his heart. "But poetry is my passion," he said. "I have been on the *Cathaoir Feasa*."

"The what?"

But Aluph didn't give Beag a chance to answer, just shook his head and placed a well-manicured hand on his shoulder. "Beag, Beag," he said softly, "look at them. Is there nothing else you can do?"

Beag looked around the tavern again and he understood. "I can throw potatoes," he said mournfully.

"Aha." Aluph's face lit up. "A potato-throwing dwarf. I think we might have something."

CHAPTER SIXTEEN

Article from

The Urbs Umida Daily Chronicle

UNEARTHLY GOINGS-ON AT THE NIMBLE FINGER
BY
DEODONATUS SNOAD

My Dear Readers,

I am sure that by now there are very few of you out there who have not seen, or at the very least heard of, the Bone Magician. It is no surprise to me that once again we have Mrs. Peggotty at the Nimble Finger to thank for the opportunity to witness such an intriguing character. Mr. Benedict Pantagus, as he is known, and his assistant, his niece I believe, a Miss Juno Pantagus, are currently performing in the upstairs room at the tavern. Let us also not forget that down below, Mrs. Peggotty's cellar contains the Gluttonous Beast. What a feast of entertainment for us all. We are in her debt.

Bone Magic, the art of corpse raising, has a long history. The same could not be said of potato throwers, one of whom I saw on the Bridge the other day. I fear such a dangerous sport can only end in serious injury. Root vegetables aside, for the benefit of those of you who are not familiar with the practice of corpse raising, I shall gladly pass on what little knowledge I have of it.

Of all the mysteries life throws at us, Death must be the greatest. In centuries past, people had great faith in the power of the dead. Once a person had made the transition from the real world to the unearthly one, it was believed they were endowed with great powers. But only Bone Magicians could tap into these powers, and to do that, they had to bring the dead back to life. Once rejuvenated, these wise souls were called upon to advise the living and to prophesy the future.

I have seen Benedict Pantagus and the remarkable Madame de Bona and in all honesty it was not a pretty sight. One hopes she was rather more attractive when she was alive. Regardless of her looks, however, it cannot be denied that she fulfilled her obligations and answered all sorts of questions to the apparent satisfaction of everyone involved. Mr. Pantagus must be commended on his ingenuity and his excellent performance. It is certainly a cut above the usual trickery that goes on in this city. Whether Madame de Bona really did revive or not, I can say with certainty that I checked for strings but saw none.

But enough of that. What news of the Silver Apple Killer, I hear you ask? Well, there is news, and it is with some sorrow I must report that yesterday morning another body, the sixth now, I believe, was pulled from the Foedus. And still Mr. Coggley, our esteemed head constable, can provide us with no clue as to the identity of the fiend who is responsible. These are indeed dark days for the City.

Deodonatus smiled to himself as he re-read the piece. "The Silver Apple Killer." Yes, he liked that very much. It rolled off the tongue. Then his mind turned to the Gluttonous Beast. Deodonatus was the first to admit that he had a cold heart—he felt little for others, unless it was scorn or hate—but with the Gluttonous Beast, it was different. When he looked upon him, his insides seemed to twist. He did not like to think why.

Deodonatus was not surprised that the Urbs Umidians were so enthusiastic about the Gluttonous Beast and the Bone Magician. People wanted to be shocked and entertained, and they wanted to know that there were things out there whose existence was just that little bit worse than their own. The Beast was certainly proof of that. As for the Bone Magician, well, where was the harm in it? And there was undoubtedly money in it. *Not a job for me, though*, thought Deodonatus, suddenly standing, holding a lapel with one hand and flourishing his paper with the other, to declare authoritatively:

"Ας εξασκήσει ο καθένας την τέχνη που ξέρει."

He sat down with a smile. "I take my advice from Aristophanes. *'Let each man practice the craft he knows.'*"

Then he put pen to paper again and continued. Just as he signed off with his trademark "Until next time," there was a knock at the door.

"You're early," growled Deodonatus as he hurriedly rolled and tied the sheets. He slipped them through the crack of the door, along with a penny, and listened as the boy scampered away. Then he went to the window and looked down onto the street, absentmindedly swatting a fly that buzzed around his head. How did they survive this damned weather? Would he go out tonight? Perhaps not. He was tired. He pulled down a well-thumbed volume from the mantelpiece and turned to his favorite story. He had hardly read more than the first page when his heavy lids closed. The book slid to the floor and lay open, displaying in the flickering firelight a picture of a green and gleaming toad with jewels for eyes.

CHAPTER SEVENTEEN

A Late Supper

While Deodonatus was snoozing comfortably by his fire, Pin was out on the cold streets wondering when they would ever reach the lodging house. Beag waxed lyrical about the place the whole way and when the trio finally turned into Squid's Gate Alley, "Home to Mrs. Hoadswood's Lodging House, the best in the City," he was disappointed to find that the house looked no different from its neighbors, all of which were in a similar state of decay.

Once inside, however, he was pleasantly surprised. The place smelled fresh and dry, and his hopes were raised even further when he came to the descending stairs and inhaled the aroma that rose to tease his nostrils and make him lick his lips. The stairs led down to a large open kitchen with a gray stone floor and an enormous fireplace on the opposite wall. A long dining table stood solidly in the middle of the room, a bench along its length on either side and a rather more decorative Carver chair at each end. A woman stood by the fire, stirring a huge pot of stew. She looked up at their entrance.

"Evenin', gentlemen," she said. "You're just in time for a late supper."

She was not pretty, thought Pin, not in the way his mother had been, and was fit to burst out of her stays. Her round face was red-cheeked and her large hands chilblained, but when she smiled she radiated warmth all about her that you could almost feel.

As Pin stared at her, so Mrs. Hoadswood stared at him. In an instant her sharp eyes took in his worn shirt and thread-bare coat, his skinny legs, his ankles poking out from under his trousers (the hems had been let out long ago), and the down-at-heel boots. She knew straight away this was a boy who was looking after himself. She frowned with concern.

"Pin," said Beag, "meet Mrs. Hoadswood."

"You're very welcome here, Pin," she said as she lifted the pot from the fire and set it down on the table. She bustled him along the bench and sat him down, then brushed a few bones and bread crumbs from a plate and put it in front of him. "Help yourself," she said, smiling. "No one is allowed to leave until it's all gone."

"It's no penance," said Beag, already ladling the thick stew onto his plate.

Aluph passed the ale up the table and Pin filled his wooden cup, held it aloft, and looked at Beag. "My thanks," he said, and took a long swig.

Just as he was about to scoop up his first meaty spoonful, an elderly man came into the kitchen and sat quietly on one of the Carvers. Pin barely looked up, so intent was he on his meal, but he held the next newcomer's gaze rather longer. She didn't acknowledge that she knew him, but somehow, after the day Pin had just had, it was no surprise to him to find that he was looking straight into the dark eyes of Juno Pantagus.

As they ate, they talked. The topics, however, were rather limited in scope: mainly the weather (Aluph proclaimed that the Foedus herself had slowed her flow, it was so cold) and the Silver Apple Killer (Beag had the latest about a body in the river—"She spat it out," he said, in his inimitable way, "as if she didn't like the taste."). Pin said little enough and ate until he thought he would explode. Now and again he looked from under his lashes, invariably to see Juno staring at him. Upon introduction she had smiled lightly but that was it. When she looked away he took a moment to observe her. Her hair was black and it fell in curls from the crown of her head down past her shoulders. Her eyes were as dark as deep water and her skin was so white that, when she took a sip of wine, Pin was convinced he could see the purple liquid running down the inside of her throat. Mr. Pantagus beside her, currently sporting neither moustache nor beard, looked tired and frail, but the girl's animated conversation seemed to refresh him.

Inevitably the conversation turned to Pin and reluctantly

he spilt his tale of woe. How he lost his lodgings (Mr. Gumbroot's reputation was known to all at the table and his companions tutted sympathetically) and of his job with Mr. Gaufridus (all were eager to hear more of the toe pulling, tongue yanking, and other practices) and then to his job as corpse watcher.

"Have you ever had anyone wake up on you?" asked Beag. "After all, that's what you're watching for."

"That has not been my experience," said Pin carefully, aware that Juno regarded him intensely.

"You have a fine way with words, Master Pin," said Mr. Pantagus thoughtfully, speaking for the first time.

"If I speak well, it is the fault of my mother," said Pin quietly. "She was from a good family, the Merdegraves. She taught me many things, to read and write, to consider others, to use a knife and fork."

"What is *your* family name?" asked Mrs. Hoadswood.

Pin hesitated. He couldn't *not* answer, that would look strange, but he didn't want to be thrown out of Mrs. Hoadswood's lodging house before he had even had the opportunity to stay a night.

"Carpue, weren't it?" butted in Beag. "That's what you said on the Bridge."

"Carpue?" repeated Mr. Pantagus and raised his eyebrows.

Pin sat miserably in the chair. He knew what was coming next. It was Aluph who asked the question:

"Do you know an Oscar Carpue, the fella that—"

"Yes, Oscar Carpue is my father, but I haven't seen him since—"

Seeing Pin's discomfort, Mrs. Hoadswood interrupted. "And what of your mother?"

"She's dead, well over a year ago now."

"Then you shall need a room," she said firmly. "I have a small one up in the eaves if that would suit you."

Pin was almost speechless with delight. What luck! "Of course," he said gratefully.

"That's settled, then," said Mrs. Hoadswood cheerfully. "Let us talk no more, only eat and make merry. Beag, have you a song or a story for us tonight?"

Beag's eyes lit up. He pushed aside a platter and his mug and leaped onto the table.

"I have indeed," he said with a broad smile.

CHAPTER EIGHTEEN

Beag Tells a Story

When I was a young lad, not much shorter than I am now, I lived in a village at the foot of the Devil's Back, a steep and barren mountain. It was a sheltered spot, with the mountain behind us and the sea in front. On early summer mornings I could see the dawn's rosy fingers turning the water to a shimmering pink. In the autumn, swollen clouds hung so low, sometimes almost half the mountain would disappear. In the winter the brine would be a stony gray and the Devil's Back would be white with snow. With the advent of spring the thaw would swell the rivers and everywhere there would be the sound of the land coming to life. When I think on it now, I swear it brings a tear to my eye.

"As I grew older, yet grew no taller, a rumor began that I wasn't my mother's son at all but a changeling, a child of the mountain sprites left in place of the true baby they had stolen. The villagers were disturbed by this and wanted proof that I either was or wasn't such a baby.

"'You must go to the *Cathaoir Feasa*,' they said.

"High up on the narrow ridge of the Devil's Back, there was an old tree trunk. The tree itself, an ancient oak, had been struck by lightning many years ago and all that was left was the charred stump. And the strangest thing was that the stump had burned in such a way as to truly resemble a throne, complete with two arms, four sturdy legs, and a high back. And this wooden throne was called the *Cathaoir Feasa*—the Chair of Knowledge. It was believed that if a person could spend a whole night, from dusk until dawn, on the *Cathaoir Feasa* and come down the hill under his own steam in the morning, then that person must surely be a sprite's child and would be blessed with the gift of poetry and a yen for travel.

"My parents warned me of the dangers. The last person to sit on the *Cathaoir Feasa* had returned a gibbering wreck. It wasn't poetry he was spouting but lunacy, and he traveled no farther than the madhouse in his lifetime. I will not deny that I was wary, but I was also intrigued. At the advanced age of ten years I bade the village good-bye and set off up the Devil's Back one early autumn afternoon.

"The sky was blue and cloudless, the trees already turning as the days grew shorter. There was a nip in the air, but I climbed in a good humor. As I approached the halfway point, the land began to change. It was as if winter had already arrived. The few trees that grew there spread their bare branches up to the sky, and the ground was increasingly rocky and bare. The sky turned gray, threatening rain, and the wind was picking up. The sea, such a blue when I left the village, was now almost black and sprinkled with bobbing heads of white foam. My confidence ebbed with the setting sun.

"As the last ray of light disappeared over the horizon, the edge of my known world, I reached the summit of the Devil's Back. And what a bleak place it proved to be. The narrow ridge was no more than five strides across and there, in the middle of my path, was the *Cathaoir Feasa*. I expected to see the Devil himself seated on it, for surely only he would deserve to sit on a throne as black and charred as it was. I went forward slowly and settled down and hoped for the best.

"Well, I'll tell you now, such a wretched night I have never spent before nor would I wish to spend again.

"Nature tried her very best to deter me from my quest. The cold descended and bit my toes and my cheeks with its razor-sharp teeth. The wind howled around my ears and whispered terrible thoughts in my head that would drive a man crazy. I was shivering violently and clinging on to the arms of the chair for dear life. The gusts were so strong that I thought I should be taken up and tossed off the ridge. Then a thick fog crept up the hillside and rolled around me and over me. After that came the rain to drench me.

"I had no idea what the time was; perhaps an hour had passed, perhaps four, when the wind quieted and the rain turned to drizzle. I thought I was through the worst of it. But then the noises started. Howling and rustling, barking and baying. Great crashes like giant's footsteps on either side of me. And I felt things too, those wicked sprites no doubt, stroking my face and pressing their cold lips against my ears. I began to think that I was truly on the verge of insanity. I swear by the three-legged stool of the great bard Porick O'Lally, I could feel hands grabbing my clothing and pulling at me, trying to drag me from the chair. My last memory of that night is the sight of the cloven-footed Devil himself standing right in front of me, lit up in a streak of forked lightning.

"I woke to the sweetest tune in the world. Birdsong. And with that blessed singing I saw a ray of light. The sun was breaking through the darkness over the sea. I felt, not saw, the spirits of the ridge flee the approaching dawn, and I was overcome by a feeling of elation and then utter exhaustion.

"It was a sorry sight that greeted the welcome party when I finally staggered back into the village. I was drenched and bedraggled, my clothes were in tatters, my shoes had been blown off my feet, and I was raw from the lashing I had received all night.

"Everyone rushed out to see me.

"'He did it,' they exclaimed. 'He did it!'

"'But at what cost?' cried my mother and she dragged me home half dead as I was and laid me on my bed and fed me stew and dumplings. I fell into a fever and lay there wildly restless with my eyes closed. For three days and three nights I muttered in a language that no one could understand. On the fourth day I awoke to see my father and mother and brothers and sisters and half the village staring down at me.

" 'Well?' asked my father, his knuckles white with anxiety. 'What have you got to say for yourself?'

"Words, foreign words, tumbled from my parched lips.

" '*Neel ain tintawn mar duh hintawn fain.*'

" 'He has the knowledge! He has the knowledge!' they cried and clapped my father on the back.

"Of course, as the son of a sprite—this was considered proven beyond a doubt—I could no longer stay where I was. I was expected to go out into the world and earn my fortune. Thus you see me standing before you today. And let it be known, I might throw potatoes for a living, but in my heart I will always know that I, Beag Hickory, survived a night on the *Cathaoir Feasa* and poetry was my reward."

<hr/>

Beag took a bow and smiled as his audience broke out into enthusiastic applause. Aluph Buncombe even stood and cheered.

"Bravo," he said. "Bravo. A fine story, Beag. I do believe that if anyone could survive a night on that mountain, it would be you."

"How about one of those songs you're always telling us about?" suggested Mrs. Hoadswood, and Beag's face lit up and he was off again. As soon as one song was finished he launched into another (what a repertoire he had!) and Mr. Pantagus and Aluph, and occasionally Mrs. Hoadswood, sang along heartily. Pin, however, was fighting off one yawn after another. Juno tapped him on the shoulder.

"Come with me," she said.

Pin hesitated, then clambered off the bench and followed her up the stairs. In the hall above, away from the fire, the air was sharp and he felt wide awake again.

"Where are we going?" asked Pin.

"Mrs. Hoadswood told me to show you to your room," said Juno over her shoulder, already halfway along the corridor.

"Wait for me, then," called Pin after her and ran to catch up.

CHAPTER NINETEEN

A Disturbed Night

Breathing heavily, Pin followed Juno up countless crooked flights of stairs, around numerous corners, and down a multitude of corridors. Mrs. Hoadswood's lodging house was mazelike in its layout and Pin had no idea anymore whether he was facing north, south, east, or west. Finally his silent guide opened a door on to one last set of stairs that led to a tiny attic room with such low eaves it was hardly possible to stand up fully, even in the middle.

"Here you are," said Juno with a smile and handed him a candle.

Pin held it up and looked around with curious surprise that turned immediately to pleasure. Granted the room was exceedingly small but, as a consequence, easily warmed by the fire burning brightly in the grate. There was a skylight in the roof, but it was covered over with frozen snow. The floor was laid with broad planks of ancient oak. A large part of the room was taken up by a low wooden bed with woolen blankets and a thick bolster. At the foot of the bed was a chest upon which sat a white pitcher of water in a basin.

"So, will it suit you?"

"It's marvelous," said Pin enthusiastically. "Better than anything I could have expected. But . . . how much?" he asked nervously.

"A shilling a week," said Juno.

He had been paying four at Barton's.

"There's a nightshirt on the bed and you'll find some old clothes in the chest if you need them."

"Thank you," said Pin. Although they had not spoken of the night in the *Cella Moribundi*, he felt that there was some understanding between them.

"You're welcome," she smiled, and left without any further conversation.

Pin, suddenly overcome by fatigue, threw off his outer clothes, pulled on the thick nightshirt, and climbed into bed. The beams across the ceiling were only inches away from his face, but he didn't care. He was warm and well fed; what more could a boy want? He hugged himself tightly and congratulated himself on his good fortune. All those weeks at Barton's with the mice and rats and noise and filth. He was reminded of something his mother used to say: "Suffering sweetens the reward." She would be pleased to see how well things were working out for him.

He pulled up the blanket and felt its roughness under his chin and was reassured that this was very real. He heard the creaking of the floorboards below and guessed that the others were off to bed too. His mind drifted and he thought of Sybil and Mr. Pantagus, and Madame de Bona and, of course, Juno. Perhaps they could be friends, he thought, and determined to speak to her properly in the morning. Then his eyes closed and his breathing slowed and he was asleep.

---

*I*n the room below, Juno also lay in bed, but she was wide awake. It intrigued and troubled her that the boy with the strange eyes had turned up out of the blue. She had not thought they would cross paths again after that night with Sybil and then at the Nimble Finger. *He certainly recognized me*, she mused as she turned over. *All through supper, whenever I looked up, there he was staring at me.*

Juno knew about Oscar Carpue—who didn't? But she also knew that Mrs. Hoadswood wasn't the kind of person to judge someone by the actions of others, related or not. She would be the first to say that there were many in Irongate Prison whose only crime was poverty.

What a strange collection we are, she thought. *Beag and Aluph, Benedict and myself, and now an undertaker's assistant with a murderous past, admittedly by association*...And so her thoughts ran on and time passed and still she could not sleep. She knew what would help. She lay for a minute, in two minds, thinking about what Benedict had said earlier, but then she pulled out her trunk. She'd worry about that another day.

Pin wasn't sure what woke him. He thought perhaps a bird landing on the roof, but whatever it was it gave him a shock and he lay still with his heart pounding like a paver's hammer. The darkness was almost complete except for the faintest glow from the fire. Where was he?

Mrs. Hoadswood's, he remembered with a gleeful feeling. He curled up and closed his eyes, drawing the blanket up over his ears. If he could only recapture his dreams! But his nose began to twitch and he could smell something, a peculiar sweetness on the air, creeping into his room.

He sat up on one elbow and sniffed. Quietly he left the bed, lit the candle from the embers, and followed his nose across the room and down the stairs. Once in the corridor it was immediately obvious where the smell was coming from—hazy smoke was seeping out from under the door directly opposite. He stood with his nose pressed against the wood. It was an irresistible smell, and hardly thinking of what he was doing he grasped the handle, but before he could turn it, the door opened and he found himself face-to-face with a white-faced ghoul.

"Fiends!" He jumped back. "You nearly gave me an apoplectic fit! I fancied you to be a shade."

Juno laughed and pulled him in, shutting the door behind him. "I should have thought in your line of work you'd have met your fair share of them already."

Pin reddened. He looked around the room. It was furnished sparsely, very much like his own, but larger. "I'm sorry. I followed the smell..."

"Ah, my little secret!"

Juno went over to the fire, took away the burner, and covered it with a lid. She knelt on the floor and held her hands out to the flames.

"Join me."

Pin sat down beside her. "What were you burning?"

"Herbs," she replied. Her face was flushed and her eyes bright, but Pin wasn't so sure it was from the heat. She reached across to the bed and pulled out the trunk. "I have some for every occasion," she said, opening the lid and showing Pin the pots and packets. She pointed them out.

"Heliotrope for good luck, caraway seeds for good health, cumin for tranquillity. And here, cinnamon and anise—"

"For summoning," said Pin with a smile, which Juno returned.

"And tonight," she continued, "I was burning jasmine and lavender with a drop of bergamot oil, to help me sleep."

"Your conscience must be pricked," laughed Pin, "about what you did to me."

Juno looked guilty. "You mean that night with Sybil and Mr. Belding? I'm sorry, but I had to give you the sleeping drug; we couldn't afford to have you interfere."

"It's the strangest thing I have ever seen," said Pin. "A body coming to life in that way."

"So you were awake."

"Only just. I'm not sure it wasn't a dream."

"Don't you believe what you saw?"

"I know what I saw," said Pin. "But I also know it can't be real."

"What about Madame de Bona?"

He laughed. "That's a good trick."

"But you asked her a question! Weren't you pleased with the answer?"

"If it was true! But I think my father has gone from here. I have looked for weeks."

"Madame de Bona doesn't lie."

Pin looked at her sharply. Was she teasing? He couldn't tell. "I should have asked who killed my uncle. That would have solved a lot of problems. I wonder what Madame de Bona would have said to that."

Juno grinned. "I am sure you would be satisfied with the answer, whatever it was." She yawned widely and stretched. "You'll like it here," she said. "You're in good company. You can have my room when I go. It's bigger."

"You're going?"

"Not for a week or two. Benedict is staying here. Mrs. Hoadswood insisted, but I want to leave the City."

"So do I," said Pin with feeling. "There's nothing here for me anymore."

"I could say the same thing." Juno yawned again and Pin rose and went to the door. He sniffed the air gently and watched as she put the herbs away. He was surprised to feel disappointed that she was not going to be around much longer. She saw him watching and smiled.

"We have something else in common, you know," she said.

"Oh?"

"We are both looking for someone."

"Well, I'm looking for my father," said Pin. "Who are you looking for?"

"The man who murdered mine."

CHAPTER TWENTY

Pin's Journal

Well, it has been a week now since I met with Beag and Aluph—already Mr. Buncombe allows me to address him as such—and it is my sincere belief that I have not spent such a marvelous seven nights as this in my entire life. I cannot recall similar feelings of satisfaction and contentment since my mother died. Father went into such a decline after that and he was never the same again. As for Uncle Fabian, how I wish I knew the events of that terrible night. How I seethe when I think of him! Could it be possible that Father felt such anger too, that he lost control and took him by his scrawny throat?

It does me no good to dwell on such matters, however, and for now I prefer to think on my new friends, for already the welcome has been such that I consider them to be just that. Juno has proved to be an intriguing companion and we have spent many hours together discussing most things under the sun until the late hours. She is extremely knowledgeable about nature's bounty and I have developed quite a fondness for her aromatic practices—they are most conducive to easeful sleep—and indeed, for her own aroma; she smells of juniper. She may be serious by nature, but she has a keen wit and I fancy I sense a growing connection between us.

Mr. Pantagus in the main keeps to himself; he seems rather frail, but Beag is a remarkable fellow, an entertainer of no small talent. Most evenings after supper—to date, a superb array of Mrs. Hoadswood's pies and ale—Beag is called upon to sing or tell a story. Last night we were treated to a fine rendition of "Old Mackey Donnelly's Donkey." Beag sang the verses to the tune of "The Wild Rover of Bally Hooley," and we joined in the chorus. It goes something like this:

> Old Mackey Donnelly
> Put his donkey out to grass
> But the cheeky donkey turned
> And bit him on the . . .

Then the chorus comes in with:

> . . . As sure as roses bloom in spring
> As sure as night 'comes day
> I'll be back to Bally Hooley 'fore the
> Making of the hay.

The verses are numerous—I am sure Beag makes them up as he goes along—but it is a most enjoyable way to pass the time and certainly takes your mind off your worries.

I have a growing admiration for Aluph Buncombe. I enjoy watching him at the table, for he eats with a quiet delicacy, in complete contrast to the others, which reminds me of my mother. She was always very strict about my manners and Aluph shames me into remembering what once came naturally to me. Not only is he well spoken, but he dresses immeasurably better than the rest of us. As is currently fashionable across the river, he sports a bunch of lace at his neck, to which is pinned a brooch of a different color stone every day. Today it was a ruby. I cannot be sure of its authenticity, but it is very pleasing to the eye. There is lace at his cuffs and he wears a well-fitted waistcoat with gold embroidery. I do suspect his monocle is an affectation, as it spends more time dropping out of his eye than in it. Aluph and Beag, despite their apparent differences, are the greatest of friends. They are drawn together by the heartfelt belief that each is destined for greater things.

Tonight there was no singing, but the conversation over supper was far-ranging and most interesting. Aluph noticed that I was admiring his outfit and said as much with his attractive and practiced smile (and when I say practiced, I mean exactly that, for I see him daily in front of the looking glass in the hall).

"Aluph ain't like the rest of us," said Mrs. Hoadswood. "Sometimes I think we're lucky to be graced with his presence at the same table."

"My dear Mrs. Hoadswood, you say the nicest things," said Aluph, and his coruscating smile lit up the room. "You see," he continued, turning back to me. "It is essential in my profession that I dress thus."

"What is your business, Mr. Buncombe?" I asked with genuine interest, for I knew he worked irregular hours—but at what?

"Well, my dear boy," he said, quite brimming with self-importance, "it is difficult to explain."

"He reads lumps," said Beag gruffly.

Aluph shook his head. "That, Beag, is not strictly true, and I should have expected more from a man who claims such learning as yourself."

"Lumps?" I was intrigued.

"Head lumps—I mean _bumps_," Aluph corrected himself. "I read the bumps on people's heads."

I failed to see the difference between lumps and bumps but out of common courtesy refrained from saying so.

"For what reason?" I asked.

Aluph came around the table to stand beside me. "There are many reasons."

"But mainly for money," laughed Mrs. Hoadswood.

"A fool and his money are easily parted," muttered Beag softly.

Aluph seemed oblivious to all this and cast a critical eye over my head. "From the unique shape and texture of a person's head, I can tell what sort of character they have," he declared confidently. "It is a philosophical and scientific matter known as Cranial Topography. It's also about untapped potential. You know what you are now, but do you know what you could become?"

"Once an addlepate, always an addlepate," said Beag.

Then Mr. Pantagus spoke, to no one in particular, from the far end of the table.

"Although I know little about the science of head lumps," he said mildly as Aluph grimaced, "my own expertise being in another field altogether, I have to admire Mr. Buncombe's unswerving dedication to the subject. Whatever I think about the matter, there are plenty of people in this city who are only too willing to have their heads read. I wish him luck and I hope they are pleased with what they hear."

"I can assure you, dear Benedict," said Aluph, "that my customers are always satisfied."

"As are mine," replied Mr. Pantagus, and there was a twinkle in his eye.

Aluph turned once more to me. He pursed his lips slightly when he saw the unkempt state of my hair—I understand now that he is used to rather better coiffured tresses—but undeterred he spread his fingers wide and dug his hands into my knotted tufts and began to run his fingertips slowly over my forehead, my crown, above my ears, and down to the nape of my neck. He was silent except for the occasional "ah" or "uhuh" or "hmm."

"What have you found?" I asked, unable to hold back any longer.

Aluph wiped his hands carefully on a bright green lace-edged handkerchief he carried in his waistcoat pocket. "Well," he said finally, "your head is what I would call dolichocephalic in shape. That is, rather longer than it is wide."

I wondered if this was good or bad.

"I can tell from this," continued Aluph, tapping firmly on my left temple, "that you are a boy of great intelligence and I sense that you have an appreciation for the finer things in life."

"What else?" I asked.

Aluph smiled benignly. "I am afraid I can say no more without payment." He looked hopeful. I felt he expected a coin or two, but he was soon disabused of this notion.

"Profound, indeed," remarked Beag with a grin.

"Mr. Hickory," said Aluph with commendable restraint, "as a po-tato thrower—" he emphasized the word "potato" quite strongly—"I can hardly imagine that you have much to contribute to this discussion."

Beag would not entertain any slur on his potato-throwing talents. He stood up and raised his clenched fists. "Buncombe," he snarled, "if you don't hold your tongue I'll give you a bump you'll be feeling for the next six months." He thrust his fist across the table and Aluph leaned back quickly.

"Please, gentlemen," intervened Mrs. Hoadswood sharply, rising to her feet. Her eyes were fiery. Beag sat down again with a grunt and Aluph adjusted his cuffs. Then Mr. Pantagus asked the question that had been on the tip of everyone's tongue for days. I knew it would come.

"Well, Pin, what do you know of Fabian Merdegrave's murder?" And so I told them.

CHAPTER TWENTY-ONE

A Tale and a Deal

The murder of Uncle Fabian has its roots in the past. When my mother said she wished to marry a southerner, it caused terrible trouble and split the Merdegrave family. Grandfather said he never wanted to see her again and disowned her. Grandmother was not so violently opposed to the marriage but would not go against his wishes. When Grandmother was still alive, Mother used to take me in secret to see her. She gave us money and small gifts and smuggled out pieces of Mother's jewelry from the house. Mother was always hopeful that one day her father would relent and the rift would be healed.

"Despite this, we were happy enough. Father was a skilled carpenter and he taught me all he knew; Mother cooked and sold her wares in the market. In the evening she taught me to read and write, for she wanted me to get ahead in life. My learning, and love of it, set me apart from the other children on the street, but when I complained, Mother told me that I had a choice—to forge my own way or to follow the pack. It was her greatest desire that I should make something of myself and I know she didn't want me to stay in the City. Sometimes she told me stories about her childhood over the river, about the beautiful house she lived in with so many rooms she couldn't count them, about the servants who provided for their every need, and about her wonderful toys. I wondered why she ever left but she said to me that there was more to life than owning objects. That sometimes the most precious things of all couldn't be touched by a human hand. I didn't understand then, but I think I am beginning to understand now.

"The trouble started when Fabian, my mother's brother, found out about the secret visits. He was a drinker and a gambler and would take any wager down at the Nimble Finger. He was always in trouble, owing money to all sorts of people. When Jeremiah Ratchet, a rich man from out of town, employed some violent fellows to collect his debts, Grandfather ran out of patience and refused Fabian any more money. So Fabian came to us and threatened to tell about our secret meetings. This would have put Grandmother in a terrible position, so my father gave Fabian what he could because my mother asked him, but not the jewelry, which he hid.

"Then Grandmother died and we thought Fabian would not bother us anymore. We moved into cheaper lodgings and didn't see my uncle for a long time. We thought we might be able to live in peace again, but before long my mother fell ill and couldn't work. Father sold the jewelry to pay for cures, but nothing helped. When she died, he fell into a terrible melancholy, losing all interest in life and work. I tried my best to fulfill his promises, but my woodworking skills were not yet up to his and the jobs became fewer and fewer and our debts grew.

"Not so long ago, before he was murdered, Fabian found out where we were and came looking for money again. My father was furious and sent him away, but he returned when I was alone and he started asking about my mother's jewelry. I told him the truth, that whatever we had we pawned, except for one piece, a silver picture locket from my father, that had been buried with her in keeping with tradition. He seemed to believe me and I was glad when he left. I truly thought we were rid of him.

"When Father heard about Fabian's visit he flew into a terrible rage. 'The gutter scoundrel,' he ranted. 'He has used you, a young lad, for his own greedy ends.' He pulled on his coat. 'I know where he'll be,' he said. 'I have to get to him before it's too late.'

"I didn't understand what he meant and I waited hours before going to find him, but it was so dark and cold and the streets are so dangerous at night that I soon gave up. When I came home I found Fabian lying dead on the floor, strangled.

"I haven't seen my father since.

"Everyone thinks he killed Fabian. I find it hard to believe he could commit such a crime, but if he didn't, then why did he leave? I used to wish that he would come back. I have even searched for him, but now I am not so sure."

Pin looked around the table and he could see from their faces that they were as doubtful as he was.

"At least now you have a job and a home," said Mrs. Hoadswood gently. "Perhaps you should leave the past where it is."

"I would," Pin said, "if Deodonatus Snoad would do the same."

After supper Pin went to Juno's room. She was expecting him.

"That was quite a story," she said as they sat together by the fire inhaling the fumes from the burner. "This is a hard enough city to survive in without all that trouble."

Pin shrugged it off. He didn't want to talk about it anymore. Besides, he had an idea he wanted to suggest to her. He felt confident enough about their growing friendship that she would at least consider it. "You do all right too," he said, "with your uncle."

"That is true, though not for much longer."

"Oh?"

She wrapped her arms around her knees and stared into the flames. "We finish up at the Nimble Finger next week."

They had not spoken of their respective plans since that

first night when she told him of her quest outside the City. He welcomed the opportunity to remind her.

"You know I wish to go too." He paused. "Maybe…"

"Maybe?"

"Maybe we could go together."

"I'm not sure," said Juno slowly.

Pin had anticipated this, that Juno wouldn't be as keen as he was. After all, she seemed to be an independent, resourceful sort, used to looking after herself. Sometimes he thought her herbs were more precious to her than any person. But those very herbs were his ally tonight. He knew that under their influence she would be relaxed. He had thought it through quite carefully and there was no doubt in his mind that it was a good idea: all he had to do was persuade her of that. Despite the fact that Juno earned her living from the "supernatural," he knew that she had her feet firmly planted on the ground—you had to in Urbs Umida. He appealed to her practical side.

"I could help you with Madame de Bona. I could take Benedict's part."

Juno laughed and her tone was playful. "Part? You make it sound like an act. You seem to forget, *corpse raisers are born, not made.* Believe me, I know everything there is to know about Bone Magic."

"And I'm a quick learner," Pin said. Then he moved in with what he considered his trump card.

"I'll make a deal with you," he said, and straight away Pin knew he was right. Juno couldn't possibly resist such a challenge. Her eyes lit up and he had her rapt attention. He took a deep breath.

"If I can find out how you raise Madame de Bona, then you must take me with you when you leave Urbs Umida."

Juno chewed on her bottom lip. "Hmm. It's not so simple. Besides, I'm not even sure I'm taking Madame de Bona."

"Still, it would be safer to travel together."

"I suppose."

"And more fun."

"All right," she said finally, with a little laugh, putting out her hand. "It's a deal."

And suddenly it was Pin who was doubtful. What if he couldn't discover the secret of Bone Magic?

It was only since he had met Juno that Pin realized how lonely he was. The prospect of her leaving Urbs Umida while he stayed behind was not a pleasant one. But at least now he had the chance of a new start. Of course, there was Mr. Gaufridus to consider too, but he was exactly the sort of person who would encourage Pin to strike out on his own.

"There is one other thing that puzzles me," Pin said. "These private corpse raisings, like Sybil's. I mean, a skeleton in a show is one thing, but a real body . . ."

"You saw Mr. Belding," said Juno. "He and Sybil had a terrible argument. He accused her of not loving him and then minutes later she was run down by a horse and cart. All he wanted was the chance to say a proper good-bye and that is what we gave him."

"At least that is what he thinks you gave him," Pin mused. "But I will find out the truth."

Juno gave Pin a wry smile. "You really think you can do it, don't you?"

He nodded. "I know it cannot be real. In my world, when you are dead, you are dead."

"You should have a little more faith. Sometimes it's good to believe in magic."

"There is no magic in this city," Pin said.

CHAPTER TWENTY-TWO

Aluph Buncombe

Mrs. Cynthia Ecclestope sat nervously in her high-backed chair (upholstered in the finest imported silk, with narrow delicate legs hand-carved by blind craftsmen in the forests of the subcontinent), her eyes flicking back and forth to the clock on the mantel. The golden hands showed half past eleven. Her friends, furnished with tea (her own custom-made blend) and cake (freshly made that morning from the highest-quality ingredients and bound together—unintentionally—with the sweat from the cook's brow and—intentionally—the butler's saliva), were gathered around her on a variety of seats each placed for optimal viewing of Cynthia. They gossiped animatedly to each other behind their hands. The topics of conversation were the Bone Magician, the Gluttonous Beast, and the Silver Apple Killer. The dilemma was how they could make a visit to the first or second without succumbing to the clutches of the third.

On the stroke of eleven, the door opened and the butler

entered accompanied by another man. He coughed quietly and the ladies all looked up.

"Mr. Aluph Buncombe, your ladyships," announced the butler before withdrawing with the subtle sneer he reserved for such exalted company. Aluph remained unmoving for a few seconds, affording the ladies an opportunity to appreciate the quality of his attire, the thickness of his dark glossy hair, and his charming smile. He could hear their little intakes of breath, and smiled even more broadly, showing a rather fine set of teeth that he had buffed up earlier with the ends of a twig. Luckily he had caught sight of himself in a mirror in the hall and so was able to remove the piece of parsley—the chewing of which served to freshen his breath—that was stuck between them before he came in the room. When he felt the moment was right, Aluph strode with enviable confidence (the confidence that comes from practicing such a walk in his lodging room for hours at a time) and reached Mrs. Ecclestope within four strides even though the room was easily twenty feet across.

"Ah, Mrs. Ecclestope," he said, "what a supreme pleasure it is to look upon your fair countenance."

He leaned down and took her hand and kissed it, perhaps for a little too long, considering she was a married woman, but that was all part of his inestimable charm. Mrs. Ecclestope giggled and flushed and fanned herself furiously, only withdrawing her hand after some seconds.

"And who are all these lovely ladies?" asked Aluph,

smiling in a way that made each and every one of them feel as if he had eyes only for her.

"These are my dear friends," said Cynthia, and she introduced them one by one. And one by one Aluph kissed their soft white hands and watched as their cheeks flushed.

"Ladies," he said when they had all settled again in their seats, "as you are aware, I am Aluph Buncombe, a Cranial Topographer. With these fingers—" he held up his slender white hands and spread his digits—"I can seek out the tiniest bumps and irregularities on a person's skull. These troughs and shallows are an intricate and detailed guide to every aspect of your personality, even the parts you prefer to keep secret. Interpreted correctly, they will reveal things to a person that she didn't even know herself, and in that way might even show the future."

The ladies gasped in admiration and awe at the very thought. Surreptitiously each began fingering her skull, under the pretense of rearranging her curls or pins. No doubt they were wondering exactly how deep Aluph would probe as all their little—and not so little—secrets suddenly flashed to the forefront of their minds.

"So, Mrs. Ecclestope," said Aluph, and he wore his expression of grave and sincere concern. "Now that I have warned you of the possible consequences of your actions, are you still prepared to go on?"

Mrs. Ecclestope giggled nervously and looked around at her friends. They smiled and nodded their heads eagerly and with such wholehearted encouragement, she leaned forward slightly.

"Mr. Buncombe," she said, touching him lightly on the arm, "seeing as we are to be so well acquainted by the end of the morning, I am sure, do please call me Cynthia. And yes, I am ready."

"Excellent, Mrs.—ah, Cynthia," said Aluph. "Then let us waste no more time. Please relax and make yourself comfortable."

Aluph went to the table, where he placed his medical bag and opened it out. He reached in and withdrew a large pair of brass calipers. They were brilliantly polished and shone in the light and looked really quite menacing. An anxious "Oh" fluttered around the room.

"Please, ladies," he calmed them with his hand in the air. "Do not worry. Like so many things in life, this instrument's bark is far worse than its bite."

The ladies' faces registered confusion at the metaphor, so Aluph hurriedly explained.

"Although it looks quite brutal, it is nothing more than a simple measuring device to aid in my analysis of the head."

He stood behind Cynthia, who was sitting quite upright in the chair with her eyes tightly closed. Her white-knuckled hands were gripping the arms of the chair. Aluph took the calipers and carefully placed them over her head at various intervals and spent the next few minutes taking measurements from many different angles: over the top from back to front, under the chin to the top of the head, around the sides, from ear to ear, from the nape to the crown, and a few more for show. Aluph was another vigorous proponent of the theory that one should give the people what they want. Each measurement was carefully recorded in his notebook and on more than a few occasions accompanied by a muttered remark, such as "Aha!" or "Oho!" then "Hmm" or "I see" until the audience was in quite a state of nervous excitement.

Once the measurements had all been taken, Aluph replaced the calipers in his bag, and the ladies gave him a gentle round of applause.

"Is that it?" asked Cynthia nervously.

"Oh no," said Aluph, smiling. "We have only just begun." And he stretched his arms in front of him, cracked his knuckles, and then laid his splayed fingers on Cynthia's skull. The ladies watched in amazement as he moved his manicured fingers slowly across her head. He stood very upright with his head tilted slightly backward and his eyes closed. His lips moved but no sound came out. He was most thorough and covered every square inch of her perfumed skull but still managed not to disturb her alarmingly high hairstyle. Eventually Aluph took his hands away, stood back, and rolled his shoulders. Then he came around to the side of the chair to face the audience.

"It is completed," he said, and all the ladies clapped energetically and waited agog for his findings. Aluph unrolled a large sheet of paper and fixed it to the wall behind him.

Upon it were drawn four views of a hairless human head; the left and right sides, the back, and crown. Each part was divided into a number of irregular sections and marked with a letter of the alphabet in uppercase. Aluph took a short double-hinged pointer from his bag. With a graceful flick of his wrist he opened it out and it clicked into place. He tapped three times on the chart.

"This," he said solemnly, "is a chart of the significant regions of the human head. Each area is lettered and each letter corresponds to a certain characteristic of the human personality. From the measurements I took, combined with the feel of each area, I have reached a number of quite interesting conclusions."

Until now he had been addressing the ladies. At this point he turned to Cynthia and looked her straight in the eye.

"Cynthia," he said, "it has been an honor to feel your cranial topography. If I was your husband I should be a very proud man, for he has taken unto himself a woman of unfettered talent."

"Ooh, Mr. Buncombe," said Cynthia, quite lost for words.

"This bump here," continued Aluph, pointing to the upper part of the back of the head lettered *T*, "is particularly well developed, as are these bumps here and here, *P* and *R*." The stick tapped authoritatively on the diagram, skipping from one head and one letter to the other. Cynthia tried to follow the pointer and put her hand to her own head and started to feel her skull, managing in the process to bring about the partial collapse of her coiffure. She looked at Aluph in surprise.

"Mr. Buncombe, you are quite right, in the area of T there is certainly something here. How strange that I should not feel it before."

"You have never looked," said Aluph simply.

"But what does it mean?" said a voice in the crowd, its owner unable to control herself any longer.

"Yes, what does it all mean?" The cry was taken up by the ladies.

Aluph allowed himself a small smile at the enthusiasm of his audience. He liked to keep them in suspense.

"Well, area I relates to wit and, Cynthia, you may rest assured that you can consider yourself an eminently witty and humorous lady with a gift for comic repartee."

"It is as you say," gasped Cynthia. "My husband, dear Arthur, he says so often that I am a source of great amusement to him. And what of areas P and R?"

"Aha," continued Aluph, well into his stride by now. "P indicates that you are an honest woman with integrity and a sense of justice. I suspect that you are highly sensitive to the rights of others."

Cynthia shook her head in disbelief. "Mr. Buncombe, you astound me. Wasn't it only yesterday I told that beggar to be off? He was an eyesore on the street. The neighbors were so grateful."

"And *R* refers to matters of benevolence, including money and generosity. You are without a doubt a most generous woman, almost to a fault if you do not mind my saying. After all, it is the duty of the housewife to be frugal, but that is where *T* comes in, for it suggests from its particular shape that you are both prudent and cautious, yet able to act decisively matters of money are where concerned."

The audience took all this in with varying reactions. It was obvious that most agreed with Aluph's generous assessment of their friend, but every so often, there was a raised eyebrow or two and a discernible snigger.

"There is another area, *E*, I was quite pleased with too," he said, and Cynthia leaned forward eagerly. "It is something that we need so badly in these dark days, in this city where despair greets us on the pavements every night, with that murderer at large: it is the region of hope. I must say, Cynthia," he lowered his voice respectfully, "you display in the face of adversity an unquenchable hope that things will be better. Optimism must be the greatest gift. Believe me when I tell you I have felt heads which are too melancholy to think on. How uplifting it is for me to come across someone with such a personality as yours. It gives me great hope for the future."

Cynthia took this as a compliment and blushed accordingly. Her friends all nodded knowingly, some even a little jealously, and the overwhelming consensus was that nearly all of the ladies had thought previously that Mrs. Ecclestope's head was quite unusual but had never said so.

"In conclusion, dear Cynthia, I should like to commend you on your good fortune and your personality. You are unique among the Urbs Umidians."

The good lady's cheeks were positively burning by the time Aluph had finished and she was quite breathless. "Oh, Mr. Buncombe," she gasped, "you've made my day. Just wait until I tell Arthur. He will be so pleased to know he has such a clever wife. Sometimes I think he has his doubts."

"I am sure it will be a most welcome revelation for him," said Aluph, and he bowed gracefully and backed out of the room.

The butler, who had been listening through the door, handed Aluph a leather purse of coins.

"I think Mrs. Ecclestope was quite pleased," he said in the manner of a question.

"I believe she was," said Aluph. "I suggested her husband should have his head examined too."

"Indeed, sir," said the butler unfalteringly. "A jolly good idea if you ask me. And to think some people might describe the whole business as *T-R-I-P-E*."

"To think," smiled Aluph. "To think!"

CHAPTER TWENTY THREE

A Gruesome Discovery

She's got one," came the young boy's cry from the banks of the Foedus. "She's got one!"

An emergent body in the river was always a matter of interest to the Urbs Umidians. Generally the victims of the Foedus's watery clutches were foreign sailors from the ships that sailed up the river laden with their exotic and perfumed cargo. These ships might have spent many weeks at sea and as soon as they were able, the thirsty crew disembarked and went straight to the dockside taverns. After a long night's drinking, many a drunken tar had slipped on a wet deck and landed in the river. And that was the end of them. In winter, when the unrelenting cold seemed to thicken the river to a gravylike consistency, if a heavy object, person or otherwise, hit the water, the splash was quite subdued. Even if someone did hear your fall, in a place such as Urbs Umida, you could not rely on the kindness of strangers to help you.

Of course, all these bodies surfaced eventually. The

foreigners, identified as such by the tone of their skin and the look of their face, would be carefully searched for gold (teeth and earrings) before being thrown back into the river, the thinking being that any respectable sailor would want to be buried at sea. There was also an understanding that whoever found the body was entitled to the spoils, hence the excitement in the boy's voice. This time he was to be disappointed, for the Foedus was merely yielding the body of Harry Etcham.

Harry, a well-rounded man when he was alive, was even more bloated in death. After he had been pushed into the river, he lay submerged for days in a tangle of weeds at the base of the third arch of the Bridge. If you looked very closely, the tip of his nose was visible just under the surface.

Harry would never know who pushed him over the wall and he was neither the first to be in that position nor yet the last. The Foedus, having held him for longer than most, grew tired of his saturated and wrinkled body and relinquished him on the mudbank near the steps. He beached not on but in (on account of his weight) the mud, creating a deep depression, like some sort of expired sea creature from a bygone age. As soon as people heard the lad's shouts, anyone who was close enough came running to see. Poor dead Harry, he had never had this much attention in his life.

It just so happened that Aluph Buncombe was crossing the Bridge at that moment. He was whistling cheerily, his clinking purse tied securely to the inside of his breeches, having just had a very satisfactory session with one of Cynthia Ecclestope's friends and buoyed up by the promise of further work from her circle of elegant and sophisticated companions. He arrived at the scene at the same time as Constable Coggley, who was trying to make his way through the tightly pressed crowd.

"Stand back, stand back," he growled. They did, grudgingly, and Aluph took advantage of the parting to follow the constable closely to the steps. Coggley descended with great caution to the mud and stood over Harry's body, his lip curled in disgust.

"I'll need some help," he called up to the onlookers, but he met only stony faces.

"I will assist," said Aluph, and he came down onto the soft sucking mud. His interest in such gruesome matters was somewhat different from everyone else's. It was not financial or morbid, but scientific. Whatever he said in the drawing rooms over the river, Aluph did actually have a genuine interest in "head mapping." Recently he had been formulating a theory that a person's cranial topography might be able to indicate whether that person was prone to misfortune. Aluph also speculated, and this was quite an exciting thought, that he might even be able to tell if one person was more likely than another to fall prey to killers, understandably a topical issue at the moment.

Imagine if that was the case, he thought to himself. *I could help people to avoid being murdered. I could be a sort of cranial fortune-teller.* He didn't need to feel his own head to know that his personal fortune would be greatly increased with such a talent. Constable Coggley looked Aluph up and down, noting his finery and monocle, and wondered what he was doing this side of the river. He shrugged.

"Give us a hand, then, sir," he puffed, as with a great deal of heavy breathing and grunting he attempted to roll Harry over.

Together he and Aluph managed to haul Harry as far as the steps, where they both rested for a few moments before Aluph said, "Do you think he looks a little peculiar?"

The silence from above was deafening and when Aluph looked up he could see that the crowd had moved back from the wall. Coggley stepped in front of Aluph to have a better look and a split second later Harry Etcham's ample stomach exploded, showering anyone nearby (mainly the constable) with the vile putrefying juices of a rotting body. Aluph, by virtue of the constable's position, was shielded from the explosion and emerged relatively unscathed. Unfortunately for the constable, Harry's putrid and icy innards were running slowly down his face.

"Uuuurgh!" exclaimed the crowd in unison before breaking into loud and rakish laughter. There was nothing that pleased them more than to see the local constable suffer such unpleasantness. Coggley was fit to explode himself. He shook his slimy fist at the gaggle of people above.

"How dare you laugh at an officer of the law?" he spluttered up at them. "I'll have the lot of yer in Irongate before you know it."

At this the crowd jeered and some gestured meaningfully with their fingers. Tentatively Aluph offered Coggley his handkerchief, declining its return, and then together they managed to drag the unsightly (but significantly lighter) remains of Harry Etcham up the steps to the top, where a horse and cart was already waiting to take him to the morgue.

"Do you think he was dead before he went in?"

The constable shook his head. "Can't say. Probably jumped off the Bridge."

It was certainly not unknown for citizens of Urbs Umida to end it all in this way.

"What about the Silver Apple Killer?" asked Aluph. "Shouldn't you look for the apple?"

"Er, my thoughts exactly." Coggley fumbled inside Harry's sodden waistcoat to find a carrot and two onions.

"Try his other pocket," said Aluph, and reluctantly the constable did.

"He's been murdered all right," said Coggley grimly, and he held out his hand in the palm of which now sat a gleaming silver apple.

Aluph took the apple and turned it over. He scored the surface and a curl of silver came off with his nail. "It's painted," he said. "I wonder why."

Coggley snorted. The Silver Apple Killer was the bane of his life at the moment. Every time another body was found, Coggley was summoned to the offices of the chief magistrate and asked to account for the fact that he seemed no closer to catching the fruitily monikered murderer than he had been the previous week and the one before that. In answer to Aluph's question, he shook his head forlornly and with an air of desperation. "Who knows? I've seen some strange things in this city."

Aluph thought there could be little stranger, or more malodorous, than a constable covered in the rotten juices of a dead body, but he didn't say so. "Perhaps it's some sort of message."

"Perhaps."

Aluph turned to the cart where Harry was lying and quickly ran his hands over his head. He was disappointed to find that *B*, the area of misfortune, seemed no more developed than normal. If anything, it was underdeveloped.

Oh well, thought Aluph. He had plenty of other theories to work on, one of which was whether a skull could indicate the gullibility of a person. Mentally he ran his hands over Cynthia Ecclestope's head again. Now that *would* be useful.

By this time the crowd had dissipated and Aluph and the constable went their separate ways, the constable back to the magistrate's offices to clean up, and Aluph to Mrs. Hoadswood's for a light lunch and an afternoon nap. And

observing their departure, half hidden behind a stationary hay cart on the other side of the road, stood a solitary figure. He watched until the two turned a corner and were out of sight, then left the scene himself.

CHAPTER TWENTY-FOUR

Rudy Idolice

Pin laid the latest edition of the *Chronicle* aside with a tut and a sigh. He reached under his mattress and pulled out a wooden box and laid it on the floor in front of him. It was a wonderful piece of craftsmanship—made for him by his father of beech taken from the thick woods that surrounded the city walls—rectangular in shape, five inches by eight in length and width and perhaps five inches deep. Pin had looked after it well, polishing it regularly with a rag dipped in beeswax. It both served a purpose and reminded him of his father. At first he had carried it around in his bag, but it was awkward so as soon as Mr. Gaufridus had taken him on, he had stowed it away safely at the back of a cupboard in the basement. Now that he was at Mrs. Hoadswood's, Pin felt happy leaving the box in his room, albeit concealed.

Such was the skill of his father's carpentry that the joints were seamless, and when the lid was placed upon it, it was impossible to see where the two, box and lid, came together.

Pin felt along one edge and murmured with satisfaction when he found the spot and lifted the lid. His journal sat on top of the sheaf of yellowing papers within. He folded Deodonatus's latest piece and carefully put it in the box with the others. Then, as if changing his mind, he lifted the whole sheaf out and began to shuffle through them, top to bottom. They had all been taken from the *Chronicle* and, bar one or two, were written by Deodonatus Snoad. One after the other they told the story of Fabian's murder. It was all there, the discovery of the body, the disappearance of Oscar Carpue, and the speculation, that never-ending speculation, that Oscar was the culprit. Pin lingered over the last one for a long time. It galled him particularly.

WHAT DRIVES A MAN TO MURDER?
BY
DEODONATUS SNOAD

In which I consider the notorious case of OSCAR CARPUE and the MURDER of FABIAN MERDE-GRAVE

Pin shook his head and frowned. How many times had he read and reread these articles? As for Deodonatus Snoad, was no one safe from his poisonous pen? Even Aluph had a mention the other day. He helped Constable Coggley to bring up a body from the Foedus. Another victim of the

Silver Apple Killer. Deodonatus described Aluph as an "interpreter of lumps," which wasn't quite how Aluph would have put it. He wasn't too upset, however: as far as he was concerned, a mention in the *Chronicle* could only be good for business. In fact, Deodonatus said he might avail of Aluph's services himself, "in the interest of his Dear Readers."

"Fiends!" said Pin aloud. "The only person Deodonatus Snoad is interested in is Deodonatus Snoad." Disconsolately he replaced the bundle of papers in the box with his journal on top and closed the lid firmly. Wearily he climbed onto the bed. What a day it had been. As he lay there his restless mind turned again to the Silver Apple Killer. It was a preposterous notion that his father could be involved!

Pin closed his eyes and tried to clear his mind. Not only had he watched over a body the previous night, but Mr. Gaufridus had been called away in the afternoon and Pin was left to do everything—hammering, sawing, planing, drilling, and in between he must have run up and down the stairs a hundred times. There seemed to be a constant stream of inquiries all impatiently ringing the bell on the counter. His muscles were tense and his jaw was tight.

A light knock on the door made him sit up.

"Come in," he called, and Juno herself entered, cloaked and ready to go out.

"I wondered if you wanted to come with me to see the Gluttonous Beast," she said. "After all, if we are to leave together, you must see him before you go."

Pin smiled. She was mocking him, he knew, but not in an unkind way.

"Don't worry," he laughed. "I *will* find out. But aren't you working at the Nimble Finger tonight?"

Juno shook her head. "Benedict is feeling the cold these last few days. He doesn't look well."

You hardly look so well yourself, Pin thought knowingly. Juno's skin, always pale, was almost transparent and the veins in her temple were a vivid blue.

"So will you come?"

Pin nodded and pulled on his boots. She was right: whether they left together or separately, it would be a shame to leave Urbs Umida without seeing the Beast. As for the rights or wrongs of it—for Pin had his reservations—well, he would think on that later.

"Good," smiled Juno, already at the door. Pin buttoned his coat and hurried to catch up.

***

Down at the Nimble Finger, Rudy Idolice, proud owner and exhibitor of the Gluttonous Beast, was enjoying a brief respite from business and having a snooze on his chair. One of his few talents was the ability to sleep in virtually any position at any time.

Rudy was protective of the creature, in the same way that he was protective of any of his possessions, especially those that made him money. On occasion, when there was a lull in business, he would descend to the basement and stand in front of the cage to watch as it ate its way through whatever rancid scraps were put in front of it. Rudy always referred to the Beast as "it." He did not see it as a "he" or a "she." Perhaps if he had, he might not have found it so easy to treat it as he did. He also preferred not to look it in the eye, for even he could not deny that there was something in there that belied its monstrous form.

Rudy had been in this business all of his life, the business of the grotesque, the repulsive, the horrific. And the more hideous it was, the happier it made him, because he knew that it would appeal to all men and women, no matter how sophisticated they considered themselves to be. At one time Rudy had an entire circus under his command. Rudy Idolice's Peregrinating Panopticon of Wonders. In his more lucid moments he remembered it fondly. He was younger then, of course, and had the energy of youth, and he wasn't quite so dependent on the bottle.

At the pinnacle of his success he had five caravans and over twenty exhibits. Sometimes he boasted twenty-one, depending how he felt about the two-headed man. What a sight that was to see him argue! And then there was the woman who could bite her own elbow. Rudy chuckled. She was a one, all right. He used to take bets from the crowd before she came on. There was always someone who thought they could do it too. Oh, the cracking of bones and the groans as they contorted themselves. But the woman, Matilda, she did it with such ease. It was quite unnerving to watch as her teeth clamped around her elbow, but it was also strangely fascinating. And there had been the man with three legs. Even now Rudy had to smile when he remembered his routine. What a tap dancer! And the strangest thing was that the third leg, a genuine working jointed appendage, was neither a right foot nor a left. He had to have a third shoe made especially for it.

Rudy reached heights in the strange world of the grotesque that he had never thought to attain. But when one reaches such heights, there is often as much chance of going back down as continuing the ascent. Rudy fell. And what a fall it had been. Twenty years' work destroyed in a matter of months. He openly blamed the bearded lady. Lord, but she could take a drink. It was she who got him hooked on the gin, wheedled all his secrets out of him, including how much money he had, and then stirred all the exhibits up. What treachery! Demanding more money, better living conditions, tea breaks. Rudy ignored it all, fooling himself that his exhibits would stick with him, reward his care for them with their loyalty. After all, if it wasn't for him, where would they be? But he didn't bargain on the two-headed man. For once, he stopped arguing with himself, put his heads together, and persuaded the others to join him in revolt. They packed their bags and went to a rival show and Rudy was cast into the wilderness.

It was the Beast that saved him in the end. Every time he

looked at it he was taken aback again by its sheer hideousness. In truth the Beast had not been quite so repugnant when Rudy had first encountered it, in a forest high on the side of a steep mountain near a small village, for then it led a more active life. The villagers were quite desperate to get rid of it because it was eating its way through the small Jocastar population—its wool was their chief source of income—at a rate of one a night. When Rudy heard of the strange creature, he went immediately to the village. For a sum of money, less than he wanted but sufficient when he considered the potential earnings, he captured the Beast, caged it, and took it away.

Everywhere he took the creature it was a great success. Rudy was not educated—he could barely read and sign his name—but he had an innate understanding of human nature. Everyone, whatever their professed class, was fascinated by the freakish. A few days before he moved on from one place, he sent a runner ahead to the next town to advertise their imminent arrival. It was often unnecessary; news of the creature's utter hideousness had gone before it.

Not for the first time, the noise of brawling drinkers disturbed Rudy's sleep. He muttered bad-temperedly, left his seat, and went down to the basement to visit his hairy charge. As he stood in the half-light in front of the cage, he rubbed his hands together. It was his idea to keep the lights low: it sharpened the ears. In the gloom there was something even more terrifying about the terrible masticating and slurping of the Beast's tongue, the snuffling and snorting, and the clicking of its nails as it tried to pick the gristle from between its broken teeth.

Rudy hiccuped gently and congratulated himself again as he looked through the bars, jingling coins in his pocket. "We're a good team, you and me," he said. "We do all right."

The slurping stopped. The Beast sniffed the air loudly, burped throatily, and shuffled toward the front of the cage. Rudy took a step back.

"My word," he murmured, "but you are truly repugnant."

The Beast looked at him with huge dark eyes and blinked slowly. Then it pursed its rubbery lips and spat a long stream of saliva that landed on Rudy's forehead. Rudy yelped—the saliva burned—and automatically wiped his hand across his forehead. A mistake. His hand would smell of rotten meat for three days afterward.

"You, Monster, are as filthy as this city," he muttered and returned to the comfort of his seat, and his gin bottle, upstairs. He was still rubbing at his hand with a damp rag when he heard footsteps approaching.

"You again?" he asked of the customer and held out his hand for a sixpence piece before pulling the curtain aside.

CHAPTER TWENTY-FIVE

The Gluttonous Beast

The Nimble Finger Inn was packed to the rafters with revelers. Huddled in alcoves and niches, men and women made deals of a dubious nature. Such was the nodding and winking and nudging that it was like watching a flock of birds jostling on a roof ridge. Bizarre entertainments were under way, weevil racing being the preferred choice this week, and, of course, gambling. As ever, the air was punctuated with laughter and shouts of triumph and cries of despair when money was won and lost. It was only a matter of time before chairs would be thrown, drinks poured over heads, and fighting would break out.

Pin, trailing Juno, watched as a man, dressed rather grandly compared to his companions, wiped sweat from his furrowed brow. He looked as if he might hail from outside the city walls. In his hand he held a pair of cards.

Pin sniffed the air. *You are losing*, he thought, *and badly*.

At that moment the man groaned loudly and buried his face in his hands.

"Pay up, Mr. Ratchet," snarled his one-eyed opponent. He was undoubtedly a sailor, with his grimy headscarf and hoop earring. The hilt of his curved blade just showed above his belt. Ratchet dug deep into his pockets and began to tip the contents onto the table but not quickly enough. In a flash the sailor had his knife held against his throat. It certainly impressed upon his companion the need for haste. The sailor caught Pin's eye and a slow smile spread across his weather-beaten face. Pin ducked his head and hurried after Juno. If Ratchet smelt scared, the sailor smelt unpredictable.

At the far end of the tavern they came upon Rudy Idolice slumped on his chair. He smelled strongly of unwashed armpits. Rudy opened one eye, managed a black-gummed smile, and held out his hand.

"That'll be sixpence apiece," he mumbled. "Your eyes will pop out of your heads," he claimed gruffly as his trembling fingers closed over the money. "I can guarantee you will never have seen the like of what you see in here." His voice trailed off, the monetary flicker of enthusiasm gone. The Gluttonous Beast sold itself.

Rudy briefly indicated the warning notice from Betty Peggotty with one finger and pulled back the curtain with another. Then he practically pushed the two of them down the stairs.

The Beast sat, or lay—it was hard to tell which on account of the dark—in his cage, behind thick iron bars just wide enough apart for a man to fit his hand through. At the front of his cage, just inside the bars, the damp earthen floor was strewn with sawdust and hay and the remains of what looked like a pig. Flies circled and landed on the rotten meat, and sightless maggots could be seen moving on the torn surface. In the far corner there was a bed of straw tightly packed as if a great weight had been pressed upon it. Beside it stood a trough half filled with brackish water and covered in green mold. Outside the cage the surface of the floor was worn smooth by the feet that stood and shuffled and scraped all day. And the damp stone walls echoed the gasps and sighs of those who came to stare and to consider and to speak about the creature within.

Juno and Pin stood behind the small crowd gathered in front of the cage. The Beast, however, had turned his broad hairy back on his audience and remained resolutely unmoving despite their cries of "Hey, Beast" or "You there, with the hair" and other greetings in a similar vein.

"Perhaps he's asleep," ventured one, a small chap with a large hat.

"Or sulking," said another and he tossed a carrot through the bars, which hit the creature on the shoulder. He barely flinched.

"I don't think he eats vegetables," said the man with the hat. He had just identified the rotting flesh in the cage.

"Well, I've paid good money for this," said a third and he picked up a long stick, sharpened at one end, which was lying conveniently on the ground (one wonders if it was not placed there for this very purpose), and, to the enthusiastic cries of his male companions and the gasps of his female, he slid it through the bars and jabbed at the Beast's considerable rear with the pointed end. There was a slight twitch, and a fly was heard to buzz, but nothing more.

"Again, Charlie," urged his friends. "Give him another poke." Each member of the party secretly wished that he had been the one to find the stick but was also glad in a way that he hadn't. Charlie, now strongly aware that he must not disappoint his friends, reached in once more and poked the creature so hard that he had trouble retracting the stick. The effect was immediate.

"AAAARRRGH," roared the Beast. In an instant he leaped up, twisted around, and threw himself against the bars, causing the entire room to reverberate with the force of the impact. Charlie and his friends jumped back together, screaming and yelling, then scattered to run up the stairs. All social graces were cast aside and men and women—they were certainly not ladies and gentlemen—pushed and shoved their way to the top, dragging Juno and Pin along with them in the melee.

The Gluttonous Beast drew himself up to his full height, some seven feet five inches, and gripped the bars with his fists and shook them. He roared again, showing a mouthful of yellow teeth and four long brown canines. Saliva pooled behind his lower teeth, ran over, and dripped out of his mouth in long sticky strings.

But now he was alone again in his stinking prison. His audience was gone with hardly a trace, only the scuff marks of their fleeing boots and heels. On the ground lay a small lace handkerchief. The creature contemplated it for a while and then pushed his forearm quite easily through the bars and picked it up. He brought it to his nose and sniffed it and within its creases he detected the faint remains of lavender. He sat down heavily, landing with a resounding thud, and stared vacantly ahead. Lavender had grown on the mountain in the springtime.

A sudden movement from the darkness under the stairs caught the Beast's eye and he growled lowly. A shadowy figure came fearlessly right up to the cage and stood leaning against the cool iron, whispering softly, monotonously, to the creature. Whether the Beast listened or not was difficult to ascertain. He certainly gave no sign of it. Then the figure walked away, ascended the stairs, and was gone. All was quiet once more except for the high-pitched drone of a fly and the rumbling of the Beast's innards.

CHAPTER TWENTY SIX

Lost

Out on the street Pin and Juno caught their breath. In the short time they had been in the Nimble Finger, a thick mist had rolled off the Foedus and was spreading over the entire city, creeping slyly around corners and staying low to the ground. Juno looked at Pin anxiously and touched him on the arm.

"Are you OK?" she asked softly.

Pin nodded, burying his hands under his armpits. "I didn't think he would be so dreadful."

"Did you see the fellow hiding under the stairs?"

"I did," replied Pin through chattering teeth. "Perhaps he looks after him."

"Who knows?" said Juno. She wrapped her cloak tightly around herself, but the cold was numbing her bones. "I'm freezing," she said miserably. "Let's get back."

Pin agreed. He had suffered many winters in Urbs Umida, but none as harsh as this. They walked briskly for a short while. Soon the fog was almost tangible in its thickness. When he looked down, Pin could no longer see his feet.

"If we can find the river, we can follow it," he said, stopping and turning slowly on the spot.

"Can you not smell it?" asked Juno. She was, as usual, a few steps ahead. "I thought you could smell anything."

"Of course I can smell it," snapped Pin. He was annoyed with himself. He should have been able to get them back to the Foedus at the very least. "But when the smell is all around, it's difficult to tell which way to go. Anyway, it's not so strong tonight."

And then the creaking began.

"What's that?" asked Juno uneasily.

"I don't know. I've never heard anything like it."

It was a sort of groaning sound, almost human but not quite.

"I think it's coming from this direction," said Juno. Her voice sounded faint.

Pin was concentrating hard. "Shh," he said. He stood and listened and sniffed. "I think this might be the way," he said finally. Juno was silent.

"Juno?" he said. Then, with irritation, "Juno?"

But Juno was gone.

Pin smelled them first, their stale, human stink of rotting flesh and pus; then he heard their breathing, rattling, consumptive, harsh inhalations. He stood where he was, blinded by the mist. Suddenly, from right beside him, a malformed hand reached out of the fog and grabbed him by the arm. In a panic he kicked out and heard a yelp, but then six, eight, maybe ten hands had him in their grip.

"Ah, what have we here?" croaked someone in his ear.

"I'm just trying to get home," spluttered Pin, praying that Juno was far away. A stooped man, with a face like that of a person just risen from the grave, stepped in front of him.

"Oh," he laughed and revealed at the same time five teeth, three above and two below.

Pin waved away the fog in front of his face and he could see that he was tightly encircled by a ragtag bunch of desperate street beggars with nothing to lose and everything to gain. Their clothes were tatters, their faces pockmarked from the pox, their sunken eyes weeping, and they stank. Lord, how they stank. Tonight the fog was their friend.

"I have nothing for you," said Pin, turning out his pockets.

"No money?" snarled the stooped man.

Pin shook his head. "Truthfully, I spent it all at the Nimble Finger, to see the Beast."

"Hear that, Zeke?" said another beggar, equally repulsive in appearance and aroma, addressing the stooped man. "He likes monsters."

"Well, ain't that lucky for you, lad," Zeke sneered. "You see, it's a terrible thing to be judged on how you look. We may be ugly on the outside, but on the inside—" he paused and

came so close that his and Pin's noses were almost touching—
"we're even uglier!"

The beggars closed in, drooling and salivating and laughing. Pin started to struggle, but their wiry arms were like vices around his wrists and arms and ankles.

"Take him to the lair," spat Zeke. "I'm hungry."

"Stop!"

The voice, a man's, came from behind them. They did stop, but when they saw for whom, they laughed even louder, for the speaker was not a man of any great substance and, to Pin's dismay, he leaned on a cane.

"A lame duck," said Zeke. "Go home or we'll have to roast you too!"

"Don't turn your back on me," said the man. His voice was hard.

"Why not? What are you going to do?"

There was a whirring and a clicking and without warning the stranger darted forward and poked the beggar with his cane. There was a crackling noise, a puff of smoke, and Zeke screeched and fell to the ground. The beggars stood motionless and openmouthed for a second, then scattered. A moment later Zeke himself came to and crawled away, moaning, into the fog.

Pin was shaking as he turned to the stranger. "You saved my life."

"Not at all," said the man.

"How can I ever thank you?"

"Never mind that," said the stranger. "I'm going to the Bridge. Is that any help to you?"

"Oh yes," said Pin gratefully. "I know my way from there."

"It's closer than you think," said the man. "I know this city well, fog or no fog." He took off quickly, leaving a trail of holes in the snow with his cane.

"I thought *I* knew the City too," murmured Pin ruefully.

"I believe you saw the Beast tonight," said the man, though not conversationally, more to confirm what he already knew.

"Yes, I did," replied Pin, somewhat surprised. "How did you know?"

Pin supposed he mustn't have heard for he did not reply. They walked along briskly, their crunching footsteps accompanied by the strange groaning and creaking noises that echoed in the streets. The fog seemed to be thinning at last and Pin realized that the bright spots he could now see were from the streetlights and taverns on the Bridge. They had reached the Foedus. Pin began to feel safe again.

"I know my way from here," said Pin with audible relief. He stood on the bank, his back to the river. "Let me thank you again." He went to offer his hand but was suddenly distracted. The groaning sounds had stopped as suddenly as they had started and the whole atmosphere was lighter.

"Listen!" he said. "The groaning noise has stopped." But the stranger was preoccupied, fiddling with his cane.

"Tell me," said Pin curiously, "what was it you did with that cane?"

The man looked up and took a step toward him. Pin concluded from his odor that he didn't wash as often as he should.

"Well," came the reply, "it's a real shame you saw that."

"Why?" Suddenly Pin's confidence in this odd savior wavered.

"Because it's my little secret."

"I can keep a secret," said Pin, backing away slowly until his heels came up against the wall that ran along the riverbank.

"I am sure you can."

Without warning, the man ran forward and shoved his hand roughly into Pin's pocket.

"Hey," protested Pin, but before he could say anything more there was a whirring and a clicking and he felt an explosive impact on his chest followed by a shock like a lightning strike. He jerked backward and flipped over the wall. He felt himself falling. Time slowed. It seemed such a long way down to the river.

I can't smell the Foedus anymore, he realized just before everything went black.

CHAPTER TWENTY SEVEN

Saved

"Give ush a shpud, then," slurred the young fellow pulling at Beag's sleeve and following him out of the Nimble Finger. Beag shook his head and tried to walk away. He had been enjoying a quiet jug in a corner when the youth had recognized him as the Potato Thrower and accosted him. The cold, still air seemed to have no effect on the young fellow's inebriated state and he hiccuped loudly and swayed violently, dipping low in apparent defiance of gravity.

"I'll show yer how to shrow it."

Beag sighed heavily and turned to take a look at his challenger. Was this really his destiny? Sometimes he thought that the torture he endured that night on the *Cathaoir Feasa* was far preferable to the pain he felt daily in this city every time he had to throw a potato. With a resigned sigh he reached into his pocket and took out a large Hickory Red. He rolled it between his hands to remove the dirt—it impeded its progress through the air—as he contemplated what to do. "Very well," he said finally and knelt to draw a line in the snow. As he did so he saw something through the drunken fellow's legs (they were widely splayed to aid balance) that made him cry out.

"By the holy!" he muttered. Were his eyes deceiving him? He had just witnessed someone *falling into the Foedus*. "Hey!" Beag shouted, leaping up and breaking into a run. "What in the name of the seven saints is going on?"

A man was looking into the river, but at the sound of Beag's cry he too began to run. Beag picked up the pace, but he knew he wouldn't catch him now. He skidded to a halt, reached back, and tossed the potato with all his might. He watched, with immense satisfaction, as it whistled through the air, spinning as it went, and hit the fleeing fellow with a resounding thump on the right side of the head. It nearly felled him, and he staggered badly but picked himself up and disappeared into the night. Beag rushed to the wall and looked over.

"Holy Bally Hooley," he exclaimed. "It's Pin."

Pin was thoroughly confused. He knew he wasn't awake, but neither was he asleep. He knew he had fallen into the Foedus, but he wasn't wet. In fact, he was as warm as a toasted heel of bread. He decided he must be in heaven and had no desire to return from this peaceful world wherein he lay. But those voices, those harsh voices, persisted. He wanted them to go away, but they carried on like a shower of pebbles against a windowpane.

"Can't you do something? I thought you were a corpse raiser," said one.

"I deal with dead bodies. This one is still alive," said another.

"But he's not moving," a third voice came into the conversation.

"Perhaps he's just asleep."

"Why don't we try a sharp needle in his foot? Isn't that what he does for Mr. Gaufridus?"

"I'm sure he said something about a quill up the right nostril. That might bring him around."

"Where else could we stick something sharp? How about—"

"Juno, don't you have something in that room of yours that'd help? I know you've got herbs up there. I've smelled 'em enough times, burning at night."

"I . . . I might have something. I'll go to look."

Ah, peace again. Pin savored it, but it was short-lived. The voices started up again and his head was beginning to ache.

"What have you got there?"

"It's a sort of potion. It might help."

Pin felt something cold under his nose and then he was subject to a vicious aromatic assault. He was brought around with a violent jolt and a cough and a sneeze, and the next thing he knew he was awake and upright and surrounded by four relieved faces. Each had a hand over his or her mouth and nose.

"Oh, thank goodness," said Mrs. Hoadswood through her hanky. "Well done, Juno."

"What was that stuff?" asked Beag.

"It's Foedus water," said Pin, still choking. "It'd wake the dead, all right."

A little while later, Pin was sitting in front of the kitchen fire supping warm soup. His head was throbbing, but if he kept his brown eye closed it seemed to bring some relief. With his green eye he saw Juno standing in front of him. Her lips were drained of color and she was shaking.

"Where on earth did you get to?" she asked crossly. "One minute you were there and the next you were gone."

"You disappeared too," said Pin indignantly. "How did you get back?"

Juno looked repentant. "I'm sorry. When I couldn't find you I just kept walking and by sheer luck I ended up in Squid's Gate Alley."

Mrs. Hoadswood tutted. "You don't know just how lucky you are," she said. "These fogs aren't to be taken lightly."

"She's a devil, all right," said Beag grimly, interrupting.

"Who is?" asked Pin and Juno in unison.

"The river. She can whip up a fog in the space of a

minute. The whole city was thick with it. There's a song about her, you know. It's called 'She Sucked Him Under.'"

Before anyone could stop him Beag drew a deep breath and launched, with great enthusiasm, into the first verse:

"Old Johnny Samson,
By the river did wander,
The very next minute
She sucked him under,
She sucked him—"

"Yes, thank you, Beag," interrupted Mrs. Hoadswood. "Perhaps later."

"I don't understand," said Pin. "I thought I went in the river and yet I'm not wet."

"She's frozen over," said Beag.

"What?"

"The Foedus. Covered in a sheet of ice two feet thick. It's what saved you. You didn't go under. You just landed on top of it."

"So that's why my head hurts."

Aluph laughed. "I bet the other fellow's does too."

"Who?"

"The chap who knocked you over the wall," said Juno. "Beag threw one of his potatoes at him."

"Caught him smack on the side of the head," said Beag proudly. "My best shot ever, I should say."

Pin began to laugh but winced.

"Can you tell us what happened?" asked Mrs. Hoadswood as she ladled more soup into Pin's bowl.

"Well," began Pin. It was all coming back now. "After I lost Juno I was caught by a gang of beggars. They were going to roast me for their dinner but a stranger, it must be the man you saw, came after me and saved me by poking Zeke, the ringleader, with a stick. It made him fall over. The fellow who saved me asked if I had seen the Beast and as soon as we reached the Foedus he poked *me* with the stick. The next thing I knew I was falling over the wall."

"A stick that makes you jump?" Beag raised his eyebrows.

"I can't describe it," said Pin. "There was a whirring sound and when the stick touched me I got the most tremendous shock and it knocked me off my feet."

Beag was not convinced. "Are you sure? Perhaps the bump on your head has confused you."

"No," said Pin firmly. "I know it sounds strange, but that is what happened. Look, there's a mark where the stick poked me."

He pointed to the front of his shirt and there was indeed a dark brown stain about chest-high.

"Hmm," said Aluph, and he stroked his chin thoughtfully. "Looks like a burn to me."

"Can you remember anything about this man?" asked Beag.

Pin frowned. "Not really. It was so foggy I didn't get a

clear look at him. I do remember that he tried to pick my pocket just before I fell."

"Interesting," said Aluph thoughtfully. "But I don't think that's what he was doing."

"Then what?" asked Pin.

"I think," said Aluph slowly, reaching into Pin's coat pocket, "he was putting something in it." And with a flourish he withdrew a silver apple.

"Well, strike me down with a peacock's plume!" gasped Mrs. Hoadswood. "Pin escaped the Silver Apple Killer!"

CHAPTER TWENTY,EIGHT

Article from

The Urbs Umida Daily Chronicle

A LUCKY ESCAPE
BY
DEODONATUS SNOAD

My Dear Readers,

I am sure that by now there are very few of you out there who have not seen, or at the very least heard about, the miracle that occurred two nights ago when the River Foedus, after groaning for hours, finally came to a halt and froze over completely. The ice has been confirmed to be at least two feet thick and already the surface is overrun with stalls selling all manner of goods: garters and laces, hot drinks and buns, ham in bread and, of course, entertainers. I believe our resident potato thrower is displaying his dubious skill to all and sundry.

But even in the midst of all this fun and games, there are far more important matters at hand. Urbs Umida is without doubt (and I say this not meaning to offend any of you worthy citizens) a vile city existing in evil times. A city inhabited by ugly, evil, creatures, some barely recognizable as men; a city without self-respect, a city that is steeped in gloom and filth and run through by the stinking waters of the Foedus.

And she is a city that breeds murderers.

It is of this breed that I wish to write today and, in particular, of the Silver Apple Killer, who has had us in his fatal grip these past few weeks. Let us consider this man, and I say "man" for there is no evidence that he is a woman or a beast. There is a belief, of course, that the fairer sex is not possessed of the sort of mind or strength that could carry out such terrible crimes. I myself do not hold this to be strictly true, but that is a matter for another time.

Deodonatus laid his quill on the table and sat back in his chair. He frowned and sneered at the same time, which required significant concentration. The idea that women couldn't be cruel? How ridiculous. It almost made him laugh, and he would have except for the pain that shot through his scarred heart when he thought of his own mother. His father had beaten him, for no reason other than the fact that his son's face reminded him of his own shortcomings. But it was his mother who had the greatest effect on him. Her torture was different. It wasn't physical—there were no obvious signs of it—its legacy was deep inside. She had persecuted him day and night with her poisonous looks and barbed comments. He remembered the last time he saw them both. His father standing in the doorway with that grin on his face and the full purse in his hand. And his mother, saliva glistening on her top lip as she spoke her last words to him. Had he really expected anything different?

"You wretch," she spat. "You twisted wretch. Good riddance."

Without even knowing he was doing it, Deodonatus wiped at his cheek where all those years ago her venomous spit had landed on his skin. He picked up the quill and started to write again.

I hardly need tell you who I think is responsible for this violence. I have long held the belief that the Silver Apple Killer and the fugitive Oscar Carpue are one and the same. It is not beyond the bounds of belief for a man enraged by grief (at the loss of a wife) to suffer a mental turn and to become, quite simply, a complete lunatic. Thus could he melt into the crowd, invisible to us all, for Lord knows there is no shortage of madmen in this city.

As to his motive, well, insanity is motive enough. But to my mind, whether he is completely mad or not, what is more important is that we discover why these killings are taking place. To do this we must try to understand him better. He is trying to tell us something. At the very least the silver apple must show us that.

It has been suggested to me that perhaps he considers he is doing society a service, ridding the streets of those whom he considers undesirable. But so far his victims have been simple citizens. The first was a washerwoman, the second a chimney sweep, the third a street sweeper, the fourth a coal seller, the fifth a housemaid, the sixth a gin peddler, the seventh a wigmaker, and the eighth, the most recent, who exploded, a man of no note whatsoever.

As far as I can work out, our constable, the estimable George Coggley, considers that the murders are random, no more than a matter of bad luck on the part of the victim, and he has not yet made any connection between the eight victims. I, however, suggest to you that there must be a link. And I will go so far as to say, if we find this missing link, then we can put a stop to these dreadful acts of violence.

My question is this. Are these people unknowingly doing something to offend the killer? Are they unwittingly bringing about their own tragic ends? Let me, in fact, be absolutely blunt. Is their fate actually *their own fault?*

I finish with some surprising news. I have heard through one of my sources that two nights ago the Silver Apple Killer was thwarted. The victim, a young lad, was actually in the killer's clutches. He was pushed into the river and doubtless his final thoughts were flashing across his mind's eye as he fell and braced himself for the fatal dipping. But Lady Luck, as fickle a mistress as ever did live, was with him, for the boy landed not in the water but on the newly formed ice. Who would have thought that at the exact moment the ice closed over the river's surface a boy should fall on it? Seconds earlier he would have been trapped beneath it. What could so easily have been the instrument of his end became his savior. One man's soup is another man's poison. And if luck was with the boy, then what contrary force was with the killer? It's an ill wind, as they say.

Until next time,

Deodonatus Snoad

Deodonatus rubbed his head. He was weary these days, weary in body and soul. He took the two sheets of paper and went to the fire. He poured himself a mug of ale from a small flagon he kept beside the hearth and sat down with a contemplative look on his ugly face. Urbs Umida. He had made the City his home and it had served him well. But for all that, he scorned her people, each and every one, because no matter what they said or did, he knew that if they, his "Dear Readers," saw him they would recoil from him in the same way everyone else had done all his life.

"They deserve the Silver Apple Killer," he said with measured malevolence.

Deodonatus shook his head violently, as if to rid himself of such thoughts, but he achieved little more than to exacerbate the throbbing in his skull. He sighed and looked at the pages he had just written. As he read through them a strange look crossed his face, as if something very obvious had just occurred to him.

"They will never learn," he muttered. "*Ears had they and heard not.*" It was as true today as in the century when Aeschylus had first put the words down on paper.

Deodonatus drained his ale and gave his room a perfunctory tidy in the course of which he knocked over a small pot on his desk. He cursed the spill and made only a rudimentary effort to mop it up. Then he sat down again and took his timepiece from his pocket and noted the hour. "Hmm," he mused. "Not long now."

He reached up and took from the mantel his copy of *Houndsecker's Tales of Faeries and Blythe Spirits.* The book fell open on a much-read page:

"There was once a beautiful princess who had everything a princess could wish for . . ."

CHAPTER TWENTY NINE

Pin's Journal

———————

It is late, past midnight, but I must write this now. I have an admission. I have done something tonight that does not rest easy with me, for it involves deceit and dissembling. I admit I shy away from writing of it, but I have always held that this journal must tell my story, the whole story, not only the parts I wish others to see.

Since I fell on the Foedus some days ago and unwittingly escaped the clutches of the Silver Apple Killer, I have thought long and hard about the bargain I made with Juno. And the more I have thought about it, the more the idea has grown on me. My future is not in this city. The only question to be resolved is this: do I go with the answer I have craved—the matter of my father's innocence or guilt—or not?

Time, however, is running out. In an effort to solve the mystery of Bone Magic, I have been to see Madame de Bona again, but I am still none the wiser, only sixpence poorer. Madame de Bona played her part to perfection. Benedict orchestrated the affair and Juno created the atmosphere, for that is what she does with those herbs, masking the abominable odors from the tavern. You can even smell the Gluttonous Beast up there. I thought perhaps she should swing her bottle a little less—the smell is quite overpowering—though I suppose I am more susceptible than most. I will never believe that this resurrection is real. My father always said that there is an answer to everything in this world if we seek it out. Yet what evidence have I of trickery? Even Deodonatus Snoad seems convinced.

This whole business of bones and corpse raising preyed on my mind all day and I was so distracted that Mr. Gaufridus released me early. It is not the first time that he has done this. Sometimes I think it is just an excuse to get rid of me so he can work on some new device. He likes to keep it all secret until he has finished. It is easy enough to know when he is up to something. He is a rather careless worker; I often find things on the floor that are not part of a coffin—screws and bolts and oily chain links and such like. I suspect he keeps things hidden away in the Cella Moribundi.

My early return to Mrs. Hoadswood's afforded me the opportunity to overhear a very interesting conversation. I stopped on the stairs to savor the aroma of dinner, a habit I have developed, and as I stood there I heard Benedict and Juno arguing below. I deduced that they must be alone because the exchange was both heated and frank. I knew I should not be listening, but I could not make my feet carry me up the stairs. It became obvious that Benedict was trying to persuade Juno to perform another private corpse raising. Juno was adamant that she would not.

"We agreed," she said firmly. "Sybil was the last one. And anyway, what if there is another body watcher? Will we have to drug him like we drugged Pin?"

"There won't be," said Benedict. "This fellow assured me that the family were happy for us to be there. All they wish is to say a last farewell to their poor father who died so suddenly. It's hardly too much to ask. After next week you will be gone and need involve yourself in this business no more. Just do it as a last favor to me, an old man who hates to see others suffer."

Juno was quiet for a long time. She has a soft spot for Benedict, and I was not surprised when she relented. "Very well," she agreed finally. "But I swear to you on the memory of my <u>own father</u> that this is the last time."

Benedict seemed happy with this arrangement and they agreed to go straight from the Nimble Finger to an address over the Bridge where the family, and the body, would be waiting. And that was when I had the idea. What if I followed them to the raising? I could not miss this opportunity to witness another extraordinary act of Bone Magic. It might give me the chance I needed to solve the riddle for once and for all. My plan made, I was about to continue down the stairs when Juno started to talk again.

"Pin has asked to travel with me," she said.

"I see," was Benedict's reply. "Well, he's a good boy, loyal, hard-working."

Juno made a noise as if she wasn't sure. "My only fear is that he will hold me up. When I go from here, it is with one quest in mind."

"It seems to me," said Benedict slowly, "that you are both on a similar quest."

I heard the scrape of a chair on the floor and I knew that someone was on the way so I crept back up the stairs and to my room. Shortly after, I heard Juno's door and before long I could smell her burning herbs, not those to help her sleep but to relax. By now I knew some of the combinations well.

I settled outside the Nimble Finger around nine, and just as the bells struck the half hour, the side door opened into the alley and out came Juno and Benedict. I followed them cautiously over the Bridge. How lovely it was to inhale the clean air of the north and to walk such wide, well-lit streets. Unfortunately it was not so easy to stay out of sight and I had to keep quite far back. It wasn't long before Juno knocked at the glossy door of a large house in a well-tended square.

I strained my ears to hear a brief exchange of words before they were allowed in. This all seemed far more straightforward than Sybil's affair—at least they gained honest entry. But how should I enter the house? Certainly not in their wake. I went down the iron steps to the basement and as luck would have it a kitchen girl came out with a coal scuttle. I ducked out of sight and as soon as she started rummaging in the coal store I seized my chance and ran in.

I was in a narrow corridor, a flight of stairs directly ahead, and I guessed the kitchen was down the other end. I heard the rustling tassels of Benedict's pointed shoes before I saw them on the top stair and, seeing a door to my right, I slipped behind it to hide. Again I was blessed with good fortune, for in the light of the ensconced candles I realized I was in the very room where the body in question was laid out. I heard voices and saw a large chest by the wall in which I concealed myself just as the door began to open.

The chest held blankets and linens and made a comfortable enough hiding place. I pushed out a loose knot in the wood and through the hole I could see quite clearly into the room. I settled down with my green eye to the hole, determined to watch closely to see how Benedict worked his magic. The body, an old man, lay on the table directly ahead. Seconds later Benedict and Juno were led in by two young men dressed in black. They were followed by an older woman, also in mourning dress. From their dark brows and wide-set eyes I surmised that the two men were sons to the mother. They seemed in good enough humor under the circumstances, and even laughed a little and joked. Grief affects people in different ways—I had learned that much from Mr. Gaufridus—but there was something about this trio that made me uneasy. I had a feeling that all was not as it seemed.

At first everything went as I expected. Benedict and Juno, their top lips glistening with the unguent they smeared there, took their places and soon the aroma of Juno's bottled potion came to me, though, hidden as I was, it was very faint. Determined to keep a clear head I wrapped a linen glass-cloth around my mouth and nose and was pleasantly surprised at how effective it was. I had always found the summoning potion quite

193

cloying. Benedict raised his arms and began his now familiar speech. I must say they put on a fine show, the pair of them. Benedict's robes and bearing gave him an almost kingly air and Juno's quiet movements lent grace and solemnity to the occasion.

I observed the trio of onlookers and concluded that they seemed not so much nervous as unusually keen for the whole thing to begin. Benedict finished his incantations and I waited eagerly for the result. The boys and their mother appeared quite transfixed by their dead father but, to my surprise, the body didn't move. Benedict looked as if he was about to say something, but before he had the chance, one of the young fellows, the shorter, leaped forward and grabbed his father roughly by the shoulders and began to shake him.

"Where is it, you mean old goat?" he demanded harshly. "Tell us where you put it."

Juno and Benedict exchanged horrified glances and I heard Juno say quite clearly, "What do you mean?"

"The money," said the second son, not even looking at her. "Our inheritance." He came over and he too gave the body a tremendous shake.

"I don't know what you're talking about," said Juno steadily.

I, however, was beginning to feel nervous. The two sons were becoming increasingly violent in their efforts and their father was now quite disheveled. His hair, previously combed back and oiled, was now in a state of complete disarray, and his collar and tie were undone. One arm flopped over the side of the table. Mr. Gaufridus would have been dreadfully upset to see a valued customer in such a state, and by "customer" I mean the body. I had realized early on that Mr. Gaufridus had far more time for the dead than for the living. For myself, I had never seen such a display of rage against a person, dead or alive.

Benedict finally intervened. "Please, sirs," he said firmly. "I must ask you to stop. This isn't the way—"

"Get back, old man," said the first son, his hands gripping the lapels of his father's jacket and demanding again, "Tell us where it is."

But the corpse remained resolutely silent.

"Why won't he tell us?" asked the mother, and her tone was surprisingly menacing for such a frail-looking creature. She took a step toward Benedict and pointed at him accusingly. "I thought you said the dead had to speak the truth."

"Yes, I know," said Benedict, "but this isn't the sort of thing you're supposed to do. You must respect the dead."

"Respect the dead?" she screeched. "There's a fortune in gold pieces hidden away somewhere and that tightfisted scoundrel has died without telling us where, and that's all you can say?"

By now Benedict's concern was no longer for the dead but for the living, specifically himself and Juno, who was tugging hard at his arm.

"Let's go," she hissed urgently. "Now!"

I watched with rising panic as the two of them hurried out of the room.

"Niffy-naffy southsiders," shouted the mother, running to the door after them. "I knew we couldn't trust you. Don't expect any payment for this. We could have the pair of you, trading under false pretenses!"

How I wished I could have gone too. Instead I lay frightened half to death in the chest. The two sons, apparently realizing that no amount of shaking was going to reveal the whereabouts of the gold, stood back and began to argue over their unkempt father.

"I knew it wasn't going to work."

"But it was your idea."

"What!"

And of course they too came to blows and all I could do was wait and watch. The brothers fought each other for what seemed like an age. At one stage they rolled into the chest and knocked it backward. They were dirty fighters. Such hair tugging and low blows and, not surprisingly, violent shaking. Just when I thought there was going to be bloodshed, their mother finally pulled them apart, giving each a sharp smack around the head as she did so. The trio finally left the room, none the poorer but none the wiser.

I lay in that chest for I don't know how long after that, petrified they might return. When finally I mustered the courage to leave I was out of that house and up those iron steps like a rock from a slingshot. I ran all the way back to Squid's Gate Alley. I am sorely disappointed by the whole sorry affair, and thwarted once again in my quest.

CHAPTER THIRTY

Be Careful What
You Wish For

The very next evening Pin stood once again at Juno's door. From outside, the wind carried the laughter of the crowds on the frozen Foedus. "At least one good thing has come from it," he thought wryly. "With the waters frozen we do not have to suffer the stink." Pin had recovered remarkably well from his recent trials, both known—his escape from the Silver Apple Killer—and secret—his ordeal in the linen chest.

He knocked but there was no reply. The door was slightly open, so cautiously he looked in, half expecting Juno to be there dozing on the bed, but it was immediately obvious that the room was empty. The fire wasn't even lit. He was aware of her fragrance in the air and he inhaled deeply. It was comforting, but then all the other smells came to him and he was caught by a sudden desire to sniff her herbs. He could even see the trunk under the bed.

"I shouldn't," he said softly, "but I don't think she would mind just this once."

Pin knelt and pulled out the trunk, all the time knowing that Juno might walk in at any moment. He lifted the lid and examined the various pouches of fragrant ingredients, the potions and ointments all neatly placed within. Now, which ones were which? How many times had he watched her with the pestle and mortar—yet he couldn't remember. He would have to sniff them out, but, in truth, the trunk was such a concoction of odors that it confused his nose. Tucked in a pocket at the end was the peardrop bottle, but it was practically empty. Out of curiosity he pulled the stopper and held the bottle to his nose. Instantly he was knocked sideways by the wonderful yet unbearably intense aroma.

He lay for a short while on the floor staring up at the ceiling. The room seemed to be growing and shrinking and he could see the smallest things as if through a magnifying glass. Up in the corner where the wall met the ceiling, though to Pin it seemed only inches away, he could see a brown spider sitting in its web. And then a most curious thing happened. The spider began to shake violently from side to side, causing its whole web to move in a rapid spinning motion. Pin watched until he was dizzy, then he looked away.

Only just aware of what he was doing, Pin recorked the bottle, replaced it in the trunk, and pushed it under the bed. He stood up, but his limbs felt dead and he could not seem to control them. He managed to stagger to the door and crawl up the stairs to his attic room. It took all his energy to reach the bed but he couldn't get onto it. He shook his head and tried to focus, but the last thing he remembered was a bright light illuminating the room. Then the light shattered into a million tiny pieces and, blinded by the shower of these broken rays, Pin collapsed on the floor and lay twitching and smiling as he lapsed into a stupor.

* * *

Someone was at the door. Pin was confused. He knew where he was, but it was so bright. Surely that wasn't sunlight coming through the window? He sat up and shielded his eyes and his heart jumped like a twitching bird. In the doorway stood a motionless figure, a bright light shining around it, a shadow spread across the floor like a dark stain.

"Who's there?" asked Pin and he was surprised at the sound of his own voice.

The person took a step forward.

"Don't you know who I am?" came the reply. "Don't you know your own father?"

Pin gasped and felt his chest tightening. His breath came in short pants and he stood up but swayed and fell back onto the bed.

"Father? Is it really you?" A sob rose in his closing throat and he swallowed hard. He stared, but still he couldn't make out his father's face. "Come into the light," he said. "I can't see you."

The man came slowly forward. It was true. It *was* his

father come back to him. A smile creased his face and he held out his arms. Pin ran across the room and he felt as if his feet didn't touch the ground. He jumped up, and powerful arms enfolded him.

"I thought I would never see you again," said Pin.

His father put him down, held him at arm's length, and took a good look at him. "You've grown."

"But it's only been a few months—I can't have changed that much. And you are the same."

And it was true. Oscar Carpue looked exactly as Pin remembered him the night he disappeared. He was wearing the same worn clothes and his face was unshaven. Pin's mind was racing with a hundred questions and they tumbled out all over themselves.

"Where have you been? What about Uncle Fabian? Everyone says you killed him."

Oscar Carpue shook his head sadly.

"I never believed it," Pin said firmly. "Never, but they kept saying it. And if you didn't do it, why did you leave?"

Oscar Carpue went over to the bed and sat down. "Son, I have a surprise for you."

Pin felt his pulse quicken. "What is it?"

The smiling man said nothing, only pointed at the door.

Pin turned and he felt as if he had been hit hard in the chest. "Oh no," he said, "it cannot be."

"It is," came a gentle voice from the shadows. "Haven't you got a kiss for your own mother?"

Pin was shaking his head. "No," he said, quivering at the knee. "I watched them bury you. I know you are dead." His head was spinning. What was happening? He backed away from the two people. They were strangers to him now.

Pin was woken by a knock.

"Are you up there?" It was Aluph.

Pin got to his feet, cold and stiff, but his head was clear.

"Come up," he called.

Aluph appeared, the top of his head first, and then his smiling face. "Ah, Pin. I've been thinking about your encounter with the Silver Apple Killer. I might have something of interest to you. Come down to my room and I'll show you."

"What time is it?" asked Pin, for he had no idea whether it was the middle of the night or early morning.

"Just after eight. Are you out again tonight?"

"A little later," said Pin. "A body came in today so I must sit with it."

"This won't take long," said Aluph.

So Pin, still feeling a little odd but welcoming the distraction from the memory of his strange dream, followed him. He couldn't help but glance at Juno's door as he passed, but there wasn't a sound from within. On the floor below, Aluph held his door open and Pin walked straight in, only to be halted immediately in his tracks by possibly one of the strangest sights he had ever witnessed.

"Fiends!"

And he was well positioned to exclaim, for there in front of him, on a shelf opposite the door, arranged in order of size, ascending from right to left, was a collection of twenty-two insanely grinning skulls.

CHAPTER THIRTY-ONE

A Queer Collection

P lease," said Aluph, his light blue eyes twinkling, "shut the door!"

Pin closed the door behind him without taking his eyes off the gruesome display that was before him. To have one skull in your lodgings might be considered acceptable, but to have twenty-two (Pin counted them twice) could only be considered...

"Fantastic!" he gasped.

Aluph smiled in a sort of embarrassed yet pleased way. "This is my very special collection," he said and he chose a skull from the middle of the row. He held it in the palm of his left hand while running the fingertips of his right over the smooth, yellowing bone.

"But where did you get these from?" said Pin nervously.

"Oh, my dear boy," said Aluph hurriedly, "do not be alarmed. No crime has been committed in their acquisition, I assure you. I obtained them from the anatomy school by the river, after they had finished with them of course."

"They?"

"The surgeons," replied Aluph.

"You mean after they cut up their bodies?"

"Yes, yes," said Aluph breezily, as if it was a fact of very little consequence. "Of course, I only take the ones where they haven't opened up the head. I need the skull intact. Once the surgeons have used them for their demonstrations or their research, or whatever it is they do in their pursuit of surgical knowledge, they are then discarded. A man I know there saves the skulls for me. Boils them first, of course, to clean them up."

"But who were they?"

"Criminals, to a man," said Aluph matter-of-factly. "Usually hanged down at Gallows Corner or died in Irongate."

"Of course," said Pin. It was known citywide that the School of Anatomy was allowed to use the bodies of criminals to demonstrate their surgical skills (or lack of them) and procedures to students and other members of the profession.

Now curious enough to go forward and touch one, Pin asked, "But what do you do with them?"

"Well," said Aluph, "as you know, I practice the science of Cranial Topography. I know every inch of each of these skulls. Test me if you wish."

Pin managed a laugh. "Very well. Close your eyes." Aluph obliged, and Pin took a skull from the shelf and placed it on his outstretched hand. Aluph fingered the smooth bone and instantly declared it to be the seventh from the left, which

Pin agreed was correct. He proceeded to repeat this trick no less than four times with equal accuracy.

"Quite remarkable," said Pin, and Aluph took a bow.

"What does this mean?" Pin pulled down the last and largest skull from the shelf. The surface had been divided, by means of black ink, into various regions and within each was a letter.

"Ah," said Aluph, "the letters indicate the location of the various characteristics of a person. Feel this." He gave him a skull and Pin ran his fingers over the part marked *D*.

"And now feel this," said Aluph, handing him another.

"Oh," exclaimed Pin in surprise. "One lump is quite larger than the other."

"And what does this letter mean?" He was pointing to an *X*.

"Rage," said Aluph. "In simple terms, it can be surmised that the owner of this skull probably had quite a temper."

"Maybe that is what got him into trouble in the first place," suggested Pin.

"Exactly," said Aluph. "You see, I wish to put together a collection to demonstrate every variation in the topography of the human cranium. I know some people laugh at me, and perhaps I do take advantage of the foolishness of the rich—"

"No more than they deserve," interrupted Pin with feeling.

Aluph acknowledged his support with a smile and continued, "But it is my living and I make no apologies for that.

There is another far more serious side to it, however. Imagine if I could tell from an early age what a person's true inclinations were, then I would have the chance to save them from themselves." A misty look came to Aluph's eye and in that instant Pin saw him in a new light.

"You mean if you could tell that a person was going to be bad, then you could perhaps change them?"

Aluph smiled wryly. "Yes, that is what I propose."

Pin looked long and hard at the skulls. "Do you know the crimes these people committed?"

"Alas, I do not," said Aluph. "If I did know, how very interesting it would be to see how the skull fits the crime! But I did not bring you up here to discuss skulls." He replaced them all carefully, turning each slightly to make sure they faced in the same direction. "I wanted to show you this."

He laid a piece of paper on the table and smoothed it out. It comprised bold and plain text and a variety of fonts. There was a small, but detailed, diagram at the bottom.

Pin drew a sharp breath. "Oh Lord, it's the stick that makes you jump."

CHAPTER THIRTY-TWO

Pin's Journal

What an intriguing fellow that Mr. Buncombe is! Tonight in his room he proposed a most interesting idea, namely that if a person's character is evident from the bumps on his head, then perhaps it would be possible to have some influence over his chosen path in life. I thought this a splendid idea in the main, but I argued that a person might not want to be deterred from their crooked path, that they might prefer to be a criminal. Aluph thought on this for a while and had the good grace to admit that his was a theory not entirely without problems. But he concluded that in such a case the person should be jailed there and then for their and everybody else's sake. I must say, if what Aluph suggested was true, then Urbs Umida would be a better place altogether, though perhaps there would be a need for more prisons.

Aluph has always seemed a little regretful about how he spends his day, and now I understand why: all these head readings he must undertake with those frivolous ladies, when in fact he would prefer to be working on his scientific theories. But we all need to make money. I reassured him that he was giving those ladies of leisure exactly what they wanted. How could that be wrong? Aluph's skull collection was not even the most interesting part of the evening. He went on to show me a most peculiar advertisement from the "Chronicle" for an invention called a Friction Stick. And then, when I thought I could be surprised no more, he produced one from the cupboard!

"I bought it quite recently, for a number of reasons," he said. "But I also thought perhaps it might afford protection on the streets, what with this murderer out and about."

The Friction Stick truly was a fascinating object. At first glance it looked just like a walking stick—one end was tipped with metal, brass I believe—but the other end had an arrangement of interlocking cogs and wheels. A handle was attached to the wheels, which when turned seemed to cause a small glass plate to rotate. Aluph turned the handle and the most ominous whirring started up and my blood chilled at the sound.

"That's exactly the noise I heard," I said to him, "just before the Silver Apple Killer poked me."

We both watched as the wheels spun faster and faster and sparks began to fly around the room.

"This spinning generates a sort of energy field," said Aluph. "It's invisible, but if you touch the metal endpiece, well, you know what happens."

Indeed I did and I still had a burn mark on my chest to prove it.

"The force itself is surprisingly strong," said Aluph, "even after only a few turns."

We were both silent for a long moment. We knew now how the murderer committed his crimes, but we were no closer to knowing his identity or his motive. I recalled the moment the strange man came to my aid out of the fog. When I saw his cane I thought it a sign of weakness. How wrong I was.

"For better or worse," concluded Aluph, "I think we should pass this information on to Constable Coggley. I have an appointment tonight, but I shall pay a visit to our good constable on my return."

I bade Aluph good night after that and left in quite a quiver of excitement. I went straight to Juno's room—I had to tell her what I had seen and learned—but there was no answer, so I returned to my room hoping she might be back before I went out again.

The evening passed slowly. I sat deep in thought in front of the fire and considered the events of the past few days. My fateful encounter with the Silver Apple Killer was still at the forefront of my mind, but even though I shuddered at the memory, at least one good thing had come of it: I knew now for certain that the Silver Apple Killer was not my father. Apart from the fact that it would be unthinkable for my father to try to kill me, his only son, there was also the matter of his height; the Silver Apple Killer was at least eight inches too short! Not surprisingly, I was also thinking about my foray into Juno's trunk and the disturbing effect her potion had on me. I resolved there and then never to sniff any of her bottles again.

In the warm room my eyes began to close and I drifted off help-lessly into a dream filled with grinning skulls and deep snow and graves and bottles and canes with wheels.

I woke with a start. How long had I been asleep? From the odor drifting up to my room I knew straight away that Juno was back. I took my coat and hat and went down to see her.

"Juno," I hissed, tapping at the door, "I know you're in there. Let me in. It's important."

There was a long silence, but then the door opened slowly and Juno looked out sleepily.

"Oh, it's you." She stepped back and I entered. The room was filled with a thick fog and I was reminded sharply about what I had done earlier. But this was not the time for confessions.

"Fiends! What's going on in here?" I asked, coughing and waving my arms about. "I can hardly see." I went straight to the window and pushed it open. The cold air rushed in and the thick smoke streamed out into the night.

"This can't be good for you," I warned.

"I have such terrible trouble sleeping," muttered Juno. When I turned around, her upper lip glistened and I knew she had just smeared it with her unguent. Instantly her eyes brightened and her cheeks col-ored. She shivered and shut the window. "What did you want anyway? It's late." Now she bristled with efficiency, as if nothing had happened, and it struck me immediately that the application of the unguent had something to do with her sudden revival. And if that was the case, I thought wryly, I could have done with some earlier.

"I've got something to tell you, about the Silver Apple Killer. He uses a Friction Stick."

"A Friction Stick?"

"It generates power, enough to burn you and to knock you over." I was bursting to tell her everything, but the clock was striking the hour outside.

"Listen," I said, "I can't talk now. I have to go to the Cella Moribundi."

"Then I'll come with you," said Juno simply. "I'll keep you company," and she wrapped her cloak around her and left the room, expecting me, as usual, to follow.

CHAPTER THIRTY-THREE

Bumps in the Night

Aluph Buncombe quickened his pace and cursed the rawness of the cold. It was very dark, with only one streetlamp the whole length of the road, and although he couldn't see them, he knew there were people watching him from shadowy doorways. A little farther down the street, a tavern door was thrown open and two men spilled out to continue their altercation in the gutter. Aluph hesitated. He was already regretting that he had accepted this particular head-reading invitation. He much preferred to go over the river. Whatever he really thought of the northerners, at least he was always in luxurious surroundings.

But Aluph was a man who kept his promises. He had sent word that he was on his way; it was too late to turn back. So he braced himself and strode on with false confidence until he came to Number 15. He rapped on the door and waited. A minute or so later it opened slowly and Aluph flashed his best smile for the crone who stood there.

"Yes?" she croaked.

Aluph composed himself as best he could and stated that he was "Here to see Mr. Snoad."

"Eh?" she croaked.

"Mr. Snoad."

"Wassat?"

"Mr. Snoad!" he said finally, only inches away from her waxy ears.

"Top floor."

"Much obliged," said Aluph, tipping his hat, and he stepped in and closed the door behind him. Instantly he was filled with regret and fear and nausea. The smell in the narrow corridor was as far from the delicious smells at Mrs. Hoadswood's as was possible. The walls that he brushed against were sticky and the floor seemed soft underfoot, but he dared not look down. He didn't want to know what he was standing on.

"Evenin'," said a shifty-looking fellow emerging from a room on the left. He squeezed past and Aluph instinctively held on tightly to his purse. And rightly so, for he could feel the man's fingers all over his jacket as he went by. The sly chap gave a little laugh and slipped out onto the street, and Aluph began to breathe again.

"This is the first and last time I'm doing this," he vowed to himself as he began to climb the stairs. "Over the Foedus or not at all." He had only accepted because he was hoping that Deodonatus would like what he heard—indeed he was going to make sure that he did, and then he might put in a good word for him in the *Chronicle*. But he hadn't thought Snoad would live in such a dreadful part of the City. Aluph always maintained that there was no such thing as bad publicity. Now he just wondered if he would survive long enough to enjoy it.

He took the stairs one at a time, his pace decreasing as he approached the top. Halfway along the corridor he came to the door, but before he could rap upon it with his knuckles, it opened slowly.

"Mr. Buncombe, I presume."

"At your service," replied Aluph, peering into the gloom. "Would you be Mr. Snoad?"

"I am," came the reply and the door opened a little wider. "Come in."

The voice was gruff, muffled almost and, thought Aluph, neither northern nor southern. The room was very badly lit: two short candles on the wall and the glow of the fire. He stood where he was for some seconds as his eyes adjusted to the gloom. The room was spacious and surprisingly neat, apart from a large desk that was strewn with news journals and paper and empty inkpots.

A voice came from over in the corner, to the right of the window, by the fire.

"Well, come on, then. Do your stuff."

"Of course, Mr. Snoad. Now what had you in mind?"

"I hear you can tell the future from my bumps," he said

brusquely. "I want to know what's ahead of me in this miserable life."

"Well," said Aluph, "I am not quite a fortune-teller—"

"What are you, then?" interrupted Deodonatus. "If you don't tell the future, what do you do?"

"It's not that I don't tell the future," said Aluph carefully. After all, if that's what Deodonatus wanted he could certainly have a decent stab at it. "It's simply that with proper cranial analysis you can be more certain of the path that is ahead of you."

"That sounds like what I want," said Deodonatus. "Get on with it, then."

Hmm, thought Aluph. This was not quite what he expected. He would have to play this carefully. He doubted Deodonatus Snoad was one for flattery. He was too sharp for that.

"Perhaps we could have some more light?"

"No," was the curt reply.

Aluph felt distinctly uncomfortable. "Ehem," he said, and could scarcely believe his nerve. "It is customary to receive a portion of the fee up front."

"On the desk," said Deodonatus. "Take it now but don't cheat on me. I know what's there."

"I wouldn't even think of it, Mr. Snoad," said Aluph. "For sure, it would be all over the *Chronicle* in the morning."

Aluph went to the desk and felt around for the money. These certainly were not the sort of conditions he was used to working in. His fumbling hands closed at last around a pile of coins. Shillings by the feel of them. He dropped them in his pocket and all the while he was conscious of a pair of eyes on him.

"Hurry up," growled Deodonatus. "I haven't got all night."

Aluph went over to the chair where Deodonatus was sitting. There was something sticky on his fingers and he wiped them surreptitiously down his trouser leg. At that moment the moon came out and, for a few seconds only, Aluph could see Deodonatus silhouetted in the pale light. It was an extraordinary sight. That protruding brow, the bulbous nose, the knobbly chin that rested on his chest. His breath caught in his throat, but he managed to stay calm.

"Perhaps you could sit forward a little," he said and he realized that his voice had risen somewhat in pitch. Deodonatus obliged and Aluph began.

He laid his hands on Deodonatus's head. "What a fine head of hair you have," he began. He could swear there were things crawling in it.

Deodonatus merely grunted.

"Very well," nodded Aluph, relieved at not having to keep up a stream of mundane chatter. Slowly he moved his fingertips through the matted hair and took a curious pleasure in the knowledge that he was also wiping his fingers clean at the same time.

"You have an enlarged sub-nape lobe."

"What does that mean?" asked Deodonatus.

"Well," said Aluph carefully, "it's a good thing really. It means you have a talent for . . . for . . . information, for communicating ideas. Do you find that people listen to you when you speak?"

Deodonatus grunted. "I don't speak to that many folk these days. Whenever I have in the past, I found they had little to say. They preferred to look."

"Like the Gluttonous Beast," said Aluph, without thinking. "What a spectacle that is. I take it you have paid a vis—"

He stopped in mid-sentence and groaned inwardly. What was he doing? He had virtually told Mr. Snoad that he looked like a creature that was renowned for its ugliness and foul eating habits.

The sneer on Deodonatus's face curled even further up his cheek until his lip almost touched his nostril—not as difficult as it might sound, bearing in mind the proximity of the two features on his extraordinary visage.

"The Gluttonous Beast," he muttered. "Aye, I have seen him and smelt him." He turned his head to cock a watery eye at Aluph who, when he caught sight of the face that fronted the head he was feeling, couldn't help a sharp intake of breath. Deodonatus harrumphed nastily.

"I suppose you think it is right for men to be able to gaze upon those less fortunate than themselves?"

"It's not that I think it is right," said Aluph carefully, as he kneaded the top of Deodonatus's head. He was beginning to wonder where this was leading. "But it is most entertaining

and er . . . well . . . there is a need in people to be entertained,"
he finished weakly.

Now Deodonatus's face was creased into a frown.

"So, it's entertainment, is it? To stare at beasts who are in
cages by virtue of the fact that those on one side of the bars
are deemed normal and those on the other unacceptable."

"Well, of course when you look at it that way, it seems less
acceptable, that is not to be doubted." Quickly Aluph tried
to change the subject. "But what of the Bone Magician?"

Deodonatus was not to be swayed. "Bah," he exclaimed.
"Nothing but trickery. He's good, I'll give the man that, old
Benedict Pantagus. But what about the Beast? Does he not
deserve our sympathy?"

Just then Aluph came across an unusually large bump
and when he probed it, Deodonatus let out a screech that
would have woken the dead. He howled like a wounded animal and leaped out of the chair. Aluph's heart went into
convulsions.

"Mr. Snoad," he said, shrinking back across the room.
"Please accept my apologies. Such an unusual bump, it must
mean something."

"It—is—very—painful," snarled Deodonatus through
gritted teeth as he sat back down. "Perhaps you could be so
kind as to not poke it again?"

"You're absolutely right," said Aluph. "This particular
spot, so abnormally swollen as it is, denotes that you are a
man of extreme sensitivity to the human condition."

"Hah," snorted Deodonatus, by now in a thoroughly bad

temper. "Sensitive to the human condition? Me? What a fickle world this is! There's not a soul out there who is sensitive to my condition. Do you know what they called me when I was a child?"

"No," said Aluph, wishing with all his heart that he could leave this miserable place and get back to Mrs. Hoadswood's.

"They called me Toad Boy."

"Why?"

"Why do you think, you fool? Because I look like a toad."

"Maybe all you need is a kiss," said Aluph, "from, er, a princess." Fear had scrambled his brain like a plate of Mrs. Hoadswood's eggs. In reply Deodonatus employed the full force of his sarcasm.

"And may I ask, Mr. Buncombe, what princess exists out there who might consent to kissing one such as I?" At which point he jumped up, took a candle from the wall, and held it aloft. Aluph gulped and stepped back. Never in his life had he seen such a dreadful sight as Deodonatus Snoad's distorted face.

"By Jove and the Olympian Gods," he said classically. "But you are *more* wretched than the Gluttonous Beast."

"Aaaahhhh," roared Deodonatus and Aluph felt the spittle on his cheeks. "Get out of here, you . . . you mindless charlatan. I might be ugly, but I'm not a fool. You couldn't tell the future if it poked you in the eye!"

Aluph needed no further persuading. He ran across the room, flung open the door, and skidded into the corridor. As he took the steps three at a time he could hear Deodonatus inside still roaring and shouting and stamping about. Deodonatus watched from the window as Aluph sprinted down the street. Then he took the mirror out of the desk drawer and unwrapped it. Slowly he held it up to his face and looked. Seconds later he threw it to the floor, where it smashed into a hundred pieces.

"What a fool I am," he berated himself.

His eyes alighted on the two sheets on the desk. He threw them on the fire. Then he sat down and took out a fresh sheet from the drawer and began to write. The quill scratched across the page, tearing at the paper, and all the time he muttered and mumbled to himself. Finally he rolled it up, tied it, and rang for the boy. As soon as he was gone, Deodonatus—cloaked, scarfed, and hatted—went out into the night.

CHAPTER THIRTY FOUR

Under Cover

As they hurried along the icy pavements toward Mr. Gaufridus's shop, Juno's eyes widened as Pin recounted in detail what he had seen and heard in Aluph's room.

"And Aluph is going to tell Coggley about it all tonight," he finished with a flourish.

"Coggley would benefit greatly from a poke with a Friction Stick!" laughed Juno. "But how does any of this help find the Silver Apple Killer?"

"Well," said Pin, "I've been thinking. If we can find out who bought these Friction Sticks, then we can track down the murderer."

Juno's eyebrows raised. "How do *we* do that?"

"We could go down to the *Chronicle,*" Pin suggested, "and ask who placed the advertisement."

Juno looked uncertain. "But the killer might not have bought it from the paper, but from someone who already had one. Or," she hesitated for a moment, "maybe Aluph is the killer!"

Pin laughed and shook his head. "No, he's definitely too tall."

They turned into Melancholy Lane and Juno slowed and tugged on Pin's arm.

"You're sure Mr. Gaufridus won't be here?"

"Certain," said Pin. "The only man in there tonight is a dead one!" But he peered in at the undertaker's window to make sure before he opened the door with his key. Then the two of them slipped in, passing the polished coffins and marble headstones, and descended the stairs to the basement, where Pin lit a lamp. Juno looked around the workshop, at the tools on the bench, at the half-finished coffins stacked one on top of the other or leaning against the wall. She went over to the black door of the *Cella Moribundi*, but she didn't open it.

"So, who's in there?"

"Albert," said Pin simply. "He's quite a large fellow, though. Look, here's his coffin. I had to make it specially to fit him." He pointed in the direction of a coffin that was noticeably deeper and wider than the rest, standing almost upright against the wall.

"Come on," said Pin, anxious to do the job he was paid for. "Let's go in."

Juno followed, holding her candle up high.

"Ooh, it's cold," she said, shivering.

"You get used to it." Pin lit the candles on the walls, and the small room was suddenly alive with flickering shadows. Albert, a mountainous man, was lying on the table.

Juno went up close for a look. "How did he die?"

"His horse kicked him in the head," said Pin, "but you would never know. Mr. Gaufridus has done a lovely job."

He had indeed and Mr. Albert H. Hambley looked remarkably peaceful considering the agonies he had endured just before he died. Then Juno turned her attention to the cupboards and drawers, opening and closing them and pulling things out and asking Pin all sorts of questions, which he answered readily, as he followed behind putting it all carefully back in place.

"So how are you getting on solving the mystery of the Bone Magician?" she asked suddenly, brandishing a pair of iron pliers.

Pin looked at her sideways as he rearranged a drawer of aptly named prodding needles in order of length and thickness. "I haven't given up yet, you know. I'll be coming with you, take my word for it."

"The answer is probably right under your nose," said Juno lightly and somewhat cryptically.

Pin stopped. "What do you mean?"

"You'll see."

She wants me to find out her secret, thought Pin excitedly, but when pressed, Juno wouldn't be drawn. She continued rummaging and eventually he became anxious. "I think you should stop," he said. "Some of these cupboards are private. Even I don't go in them."

"OK," said Juno, "but look at this. It wasn't in the cupboard; I found it behind it."

She held out the glittering contraption and Pin paled and took a step back.

"What is it?" asked Juno. "What's wrong?"

Pin felt his heart constrict in his ribs.

"Fiends!" he whispered. "It's a Friction Stick."

For a second they were both silent, each realizing at the same time what this unwitting discovery might mean. "Oh Lord," said Juno quietly. "Do you think—"

But before she could finish her question they both looked up at the sound of footsteps crossing the floor above.

"Mr. Gaufridus," hissed Pin. "It has to be. Quick. We must hide."

Pin grabbed at Juno's arm, pulled her into the workshop, and dragged her into the nearest coffin, coincidentally Mr. Albert H. Hambley's, managing to slide the lid into place just as the door swung open.

Out of all the coffins in the room to use as a hiding place, Pin had certainly chosen the best. Its generous sizing meant that he and Juno fitted in quite comfortably side by side. The lid was a tight fit but Pin sent up a silent prayer of thanks that he had taken the time earlier that day to drill the holes for the nameplate and the handles. Not only did they provide a stream of refreshing cold air, but also he and Juno could see out into the workshop.

Mr. Gaufridus did indeed enter the room and began to engage in some of those activities that people prefer to do when they think they are on their own. He picked his nose and then he scratched under his arm and tugged at his underwear, which had been causing him some trouble these last few days. But once he had adjusted himself to his satisfaction, he went straight into the *Cella Moribundi.*

"Pin," he called, "are you in there?" The door closed behind him.

"I think I'm going to sneeze," whispered Juno. "It's so dusty."

Pin rummaged in his pocket and found his handkerchief.

"Cover your nose with this," he said and handed it to her in the darkness.

"Can we escape?" Juno's voice was low and muffled.

"I don't know if we have time."

Pin was right, for Mr. Gaufridus emerged at that very moment carrying what was unmistakably the Friction Stick. Pin felt Juno's hand tighten around his and knew that she had seen it too. Mr. Gaufridus stood right in front of the coffin and, although his expression gave nothing away, Pin suspected that he was wondering why the lid was on. Juno squeezed her eyes tightly shut, anticipating the removal of the lid, but Mr. Gaufridus merely shook his head and went to the workbench, where he examined the stick carefully. Then he held it up and turned the handle and Pin and Juno watched in horror as sparks began to fly around the room. Whatever doubts they might have had were gone in an instant. Each was now utterly convinced that they were in the same room as the Silver Apple Killer.

Then the unthinkable happened. Pin coughed. A small cough, hardly discernible in fact. Mr. Gaufridus didn't even hear it. Neither did he hear the second. It was the third cough, the loudest, that caused all the trouble.

Mr. Gaufridus froze on the spot and looked straight at the coffin. He approached slowly, brandishing the Friction Stick. Inside their morbid hiding place Pin and Juno were completely helpless. Mr. Gaufridus came closer and closer. Pin waited until he was only a footstep away, then shoved the lid violently outward with his foot. Mr. Gaufridus fell backward against the bench and, for the first time since he had known him, Pin thought that he looked ever so slightly surprised.

"Run," shouted Pin, hauling Juno out by her cloak. "Run for your life!"

A couple of streets away Aluph Buncombe was also in something of a hurry. He was wagging his finger and talking crossly to himself. "Never again," he said over and over. "Never again." All thoughts of visiting Coggley were gone from his mind as he turned into Squid's Gate Alley and practically ran to the lodging house. As he let himself in, he thought he hadn't ever been so glad to step inside that door as he was at that very moment. He took the stairs in four strides and rushed into the kitchen. As one, Beag, Benedict, and Mrs. Hoadswood looked up.

"By Jove," cried Aluph with relief, "I'm glad to see you all."

"Mr. Buncombe," exclaimed Mrs. Hoadswood, "are you all right?"

"Perhaps he told one of his lovely ladies the truth for once," began Beag, who was picking at the remains of a platter of pork, but when he saw his friend's state of disarray and the expression on his face he stopped.

Aluph slumped dramatically across the table. "If only it was a lovely lady, Beag," he said. "If only! The time I've had, you wouldn't believe it."

"Tell all," said Benedict, leaning forward from his chair by the fire. "We like a good story in this house."

"Well," said Aluph as he shrugged off his long coat and placed it carefully over the back of a chair (whatever the circumstances he never draped, always folded), "I received an invitation from, of all people, Deodonatus Snoad. He wanted me to read his head. I accepted, of course. I thought it might be interesting. But now I think I am lucky to have got out of there alive. The man is a lunatic."

"Hmm," mused Beag, "I had always thought him a little eccentric perhaps, but a lunatic? Perhaps he hides his true self behind the written word."

"You should just be grateful that he hides *himself*," said Aluph with feeling and a visible shudder.

"What do you mean?" asked Mrs. Hoadswood, halting her stirring.

Aluph adjusted his necktie. "Well, he's an odd chap if ever I saw one. He keeps his room dark and covers himself up, but I soon found out why. The man is a monster. He belongs in the same cage as the Gluttonous Beast." He wiped his hand across his brow rather dramatically, leaving a shining streak across his forehead.

"What's that on your head?" asked Benedict.

Mrs. Hoadswood came over for a closer look. "It's all over your trouser leg too."

"I think it's ink," said Aluph dismissively, anxious to continue with his tale of woe. "Such an unpleasant man." But before he could go on, there was a terrible crashing and banging upstairs and seconds later Juno came rushing in.

"Help! I need help! Pin's being attacked by the Silver Apple Killer."

The kitchen emptied in seconds. Everyone ran out onto the street where, sure enough, Pin was on the ground grappling with Mr. Gaufridus. Beag dived in and took his arms and Aluph managed a leg. Pin jumped to his feet and stood over his employer, who looked a little confused (or was it angry?), holding the Friction Stick an inch away from Mr. Gaufridus's nose.

"Behold!" proclaimed Pin with the sort of flourish Aluph would gladly have employed over the river. "The Silver Apple Killer."

Mr. Gaufridus struggled to raise himself off the ground.

"If I could just speak for a moment," he spluttered. "Perhaps I can explain."

Beag eyed him, a lethal potato in his hand. "Go on."

"I'm not the killer," insisted Mr. Gaufridus. "I *make* the Friction Sticks."

CHAPTER THIRTY FIVE

Revelation

hortly afterward Mr. Gaufridus was seated at Mrs. Hoadswood's table enjoying her generous hospitality. He was still panting from the effort of chasing Pin and Juno all the way to Squid's Gate Alley, not to mention the wrestling match in the snow. Pin, Beag, Juno, and Aluph had all apologized, and Mr. Gaufridus had been most gracious, if deadpan, in his acceptance. Benedict, who had not actually taken part in the capture, merely watching from the sidelines, was examining the Friction Stick.

"That's an old one," said Mr. Gaufridus, setting down his ale. "I made it as an aid to my work. But then I thought it might have other uses, so I decided to sell them through the *Chronicle.* It was only this evening that I realized perhaps the two, the Friction Stick and the Silver Apple Killer, might be connected. That's why I came back to the shop."

"How many have you sold?" asked Aluph.

"Oh, not many," said Mr. Gaufridus. "Three or four perhaps, but I cannot tell you to whom."

"Why ever not?" asked Pin in despair. "One of your customers must be the Silver Apple Killer."

"I know why not," said Aluph slowly. "The Friction Sticks
are sold via the *Chronicle*. When I purchased mine I left the
cash and was given a ticket. All I had to do to collect the
stick was to hand over the ticket. I never gave my name."

"And if you were intending to use it for murder, you
wouldn't have given your real name anyway," said Benedict.
"How disappointing."

Mr. Gaufridus stood up and brushed himself down. "I'm
sorry I can't be of more help."

"Oh, it's been a night and a half," said Mrs. Hoadswood.
"Poor Mr. Buncombe has had a terrible time too."

Pin looked at Aluph, noticing for the first time how disheveled he was. And what was that glistening streak across
his forehead?

"Oh yes," said Aluph, ready to take up exactly where
he left off previously. "I was with your friend Deodonatus
Snoad."

"He's no friend of mine," snorted Pin, still staring intently at Aluph's forehead.

"I went to read his bumps," continued Aluph, "and what
an unpleasant experience that was. He had the most peculiar lump on the side of his head, enormous."

Beag looked at Pin and then at Aluph and then at Pin
again. It was as if a light had come on in his head. "By the
holy!" he exclaimed.

"Fiends!" said Pin simultaneously.

"Aluph, where exactly was this lump?" asked Beag.

"On his head, I told you." Aluph was a little irritated by these interruptions.

"Right or left?" asked Pin urgently.

Mrs. Hoadswood looked up from her pot and Benedict set down the Friction Stick.

Aluph thought for moment. "On the right."

"Your right or his right?"

"Both," said Aluph. "I was behind him. Why?"

"My potato," breathed Beag triumphantly.

Pin reached out and ran his finger across Aluph's forehead and held it up in front of him. "And look—"

"By Jove," whispered Aluph, and his face drained, "and by Zeus."

For Pin's finger gleamed with silver.

CHAPTER THIRTY SIX

"Nature Creates Nothing Without a Purpose"
—Aristotle

Deodonatus Snoad pulled his cloak tight at the neck and wrapped his scarf around his face. His hat was right down over his ears. The wind had taken on an almost evil chill that cut through bare skin and froze your bones to the marrow. The snow had turned to solid ice on the pavements and the soupy sludge that normally ran slowly down the center of the road had, like the Foedus, thickened with the cold so much that it no longer flowed.

"Lord above," muttered Deodonatus, and his breath froze instantly on the inside of his scarf. Despite such an exhortation, it would be wrong to think that Deodonatus had any belief in a Higher Being. He had concluded long ago that life as he knew it proved without a doubt that God did not exist. Human existence was merely a pot of random luck from which was ladled, with complete disinterest, a spoonful of good, bad, or indifferent.

It was Aluph Buncombe who had helped him decide in

the end. He didn't quite know what had come over him, to show himself to a fool like Buncombe. It was a long time since he had revealed himself in such a way. *I suppose I just wanted to know for sure*, he thought sadly, *to see whether anything had changed.*

He scurried along, a little like a rat, close to the wall and then crossed the road to the Bridge and went on to the Nimble Finger. He walked quickly across the back of the inn, stopping only to loosen his scarf before addressing Rudy Idolice, who sat as usual in his chair beside the curtain.

"I'm here to see the Gluttonous Beast."

Rudy, half asleep, didn't look up. "That'll be sixpence."

"I do not have to pay," said Deodonatus quietly.

"Wot?" Now Rudy was wide awake. He shuffled upright in the chair. "Oh, it's you. Same difference. Everyone has to pay, no matter how often you've been."

"But I'm your best customer," said Deodonatus throatily. "You've benefited greatly from me—now it's my turn, don't you think, my old friend?" He pulled aside his scarf and grabbed Rudy by the throat, drawing him up to his face. Rudy was rendered momentarily speechless, then his eyes grew wide and his befuddled brain cleared.

"Bloody 'ell," he said. "It's Mr. Hideous!"

Deodonatus smiled crookedly and with his free hand he reached into Rudy's waistcoat pocket and withdrew a large iron key. Then he threw Rudy roughly to the floor, where he lay quite still, and descended into the cellar.

Deodonatus was awash with a feeling of something like contentment, as if he had come to the end of a long journey. He knew that what he was about to see was far more repulsive than he ever was (at least that was what he liked to think: Aluph's inadvertent comparison had upset him quite badly). He could hear the snuffling of the Beast in the darkness. He went to the front of the cage and looked in. The Beast was at the back. Deodonatus began talking to him softly, and slowly the creature shuffled forward, a bone in one hand, a piece of meat in the other, and a mouthful of something else. He came forward, stopping a foot or two short of the bars, and looked straight at Deodonatus, sniffing the air like a dog.

"Hello, my old friend," said Deodonatus softly. "I've got good news. After all these weeks of coming in here to see you, to bring you some comfort, I finally know what I've got to do. I'm only sorry it's taken so long. You see, I know how you feel. Haven't I been in a cage myself? Trapped behind bars not of my own making. I've tried to help you, in my own way, but I made a mistake. I could have gone on forever. Those people out there, they are never going to understand. They could fall into the Foedus one and all and still they wouldn't know why. But it doesn't matter now. Tonight your torture is over. I am going to save you. You will be free to avenge your tormentors."

He took the key and placed it in the lock. The Beast's ears pricked up at the sound and his heart quickened. He sidled right up to the front of the cage, to face this man who had tormented him with his whispering for so long. Then, choosing his moment, with lightning speed he pushed his arm through the bars and took Deodonatus's stubby neck in his hand and squeezed it the way he squeezed flesh off a bone. When he finally let go, Deodonatus Snoad slid down the outside of the cage and lay deathly still.

The Gluttonous Beast wasted no time. How often he had dreamed of this! Bending his wrist he deftly turned the key and opened the door. He knelt beside his motionless tormentor and took his scarf and wrapped it around his own neck. Next he yanked off the hat and put it on his own head, pulling it down until it fitted tightly and tucking his ears in. With a little more difficulty he relieved Deodonatus of his cloak and wrestled it awkwardly over his shoulders. He looked down at Deodonatus and reached out to touch his glistening silver hair. Then he looked up the stairs and stretched his lips in what could only be described as a sly grin.

Shortly afterward the Gluttonous Beast slipped quietly through the tavern. He paid no attention to the crowds in the bar, and they paid no attention to him. Outside on the pavement he stopped and sniffed the air. How refreshing it was. All that talk of the stinking river, he could hardly smell it at all! He turned into the alley at the side of the Nimble Finger and loped, quite gracefully, it must be said, toward the river. Then, remarkably nimbly for a beast of his size and girth, he leaped over the wall, turning on one hand to drop lightly onto the ice. Then with barely a backward glance he slid away on his flat leathery feet toward the coast, using Deodonatus's cane as a sort of ski stick.

CHAPTER THIRTY SEVEN

Pin's Journal

*S*omething utterly dreadful has happened, a betrayal of the very worst kind. I can still hardly believe it. Juno has gone and right now I am so full of hate for her that I don't know what I would do if she returned. But I vow to find her, even if she has left this city. For I have to know if it's true.

The last time I saw her was in the kitchen when she gave me my handkerchief back.

"And this is yours too," she said, handing me a small white flower. "It was in your hanky."

I was a little embarrassed. "It's one of the flowers I found on my mother's grave," I explained. "I put them in my pocket and forgot about them."

I remember thinking at the time that she looked at me strangely. I thought she was going to say something else, but then Aluph started talking about Deodonatus and I turned to listen. By the time he finished his remarkable account Juno was gone.

I went to her room, but there was no sign of her. I looked under the bed and was shocked to see that her trunk was gone too. I could think of only one reason why she would take it: she was not coming back. I sat down, utterly confused. Only an hour or two earlier, at Mr. Gaufridus's, she seemed to hint that she wanted the two of us to travel together. And now this. Perhaps she discovered I had looked in her trunk, but surely she would have talked to me first, not just taken off.

As I sat there a movement up in the corner caught my eye. It was the brown spider and he was shaking his web as manically as ever. I had thought him merely part of my dream after I sniffed the potion. Maybe it's Juno's herbs, I mused. They've addled his brains.

And that was the moment when everything began to fall into place.

"The potion!" I shouted, jumping to my feet. "The potion in the peardrop bottle. It makes you see things."

It explained everything. The potion made me see my father and my mother although I knew it couldn't be real. Sybil and Madame de Bona, they came to life because Juno had swung the potion around the room. But what about the old man over the river, why didn't I see him revive? Because I was hidden in the linen chest. I had a cloth around my mouth and nose so I couldn't smell the potion.

The brothers smelt it, though, and the mother. And they thought their father had come back to life. They asked him about money, but it was <u>Juno's</u> voice I heard in reply, because she was the voice of the dead. And of course she didn't know where the money was.

The answers were coming thick and fast now. What of the unguent? What part did it play? I remembered how it cleared Juno's head earlier this evening. "Of course," I said out loud. "They use it to protect themselves from the effects of the potion."

I laughed. It was all so simple. Juno was right: the answer really was under my nose all the time.

Now that I had solved the puzzle, I was even more anxious to see her. Despite her absence I could still smell her; the scent of juniper was strong in the room, suspiciously so, I thought. In fact, easily as strong as when she was with me. I sniffed again and followed my nose, like a dog, down to the floor. It was definitely at its most pungent under the bed and when I saw the string I knew why. I pulled it out and held it up and looked at the tarnished locket that swung before me. I opened it with my fingernail and saw within the yellow juniper unguent. I sniffed it cautiously and in an instant my head cleared and everything around me was as sharp as a newly cut quill.

"Where have you gone?" I whispered as I turned the locket over in my hand. There were two letters engraved on the back.

And that was when I was fit to kill her.

CHAPTER THIRTY-EIGHT

A Difficult Task

It hadn't snowed for some time, but the skies were gray and heavy overhead, and evidence of the earlier scuffle outside the lodging house was still visible. As was the set of footprints that led away from the house. Pin knew instinctively that they were Juno's.

Grim-faced he followed them, toward the Bridge—it wouldn't surprise him if they led out of the City—but then the trail turned in the other direction. It started to snow lightly and Pin cursed under his breath. He had to hurry. Soon he wouldn't be able to see the prints at all. He followed them all the way to Hollow Lane, where they led him right up to the churchyard gates.

Pin watched as Juno scraped uselessly at the frozen earth around his mother's grave. Her trunk and a brown bag lay on the ground beside her. His heart was like a rock and his jaw was set firm. Every muscle in his body was taut.

"Juno."

Startled, she dropped the spade and turned her head quickly. When she saw him she looked shocked. She got to her feet.

"What are you doing here?"

"I could ask you the same thing," said Pin. "As for me, I came to tell you that I've found out your secret. It's the potion, isn't it? It makes you see what you want to see. And the juniper unguent, in the locket, it clears your head. That's why you use it, you and Benedict, isn't it?"

"Yes," said Juno.

"So why did you run off like that? And what are you doing here?"

"It's not what you think," said Juno, confused by the harshness of his tone. "I can explain it all." Her face was ghostly, her hands were trembling.

"I thought you were my friend."

"I am your friend. That's why I'm here. Can't you see? I'm trying to make it right."

"How can you make it right?"

"By putting things back where they were."

"How can you do that when I have it?"

Juno looked thoroughly bewildered. "Pin, what are you talking about?"

"The locket, you fool. *The one you stole from my own mother's grave.*" And he pulled it from his pocket and swung it in front of her. "What happened to the silver chain? Did you sell it?"

Juno's hand went automatically to her neck even though she knew the string would not be there. "My locket! Where did you find it?"

"*Your* locket?" Pin almost spat with fury. "This is my mother's locket. You stole it from her dead neck. I can't believe it, you're just a lousy grave robber."

"But it's mine," insisted Juno. "Look at the back."

Pin held up the locket and there, clearly visible in the moonlight, were the initials J C.

"They're my mother's initials," he said. "Jocelyn Carpue."

Juno stared him straight in the face. "Or Juno Catchpole." Her voice was cold and low.

Pin sneered. "Your name is Juno Pantagus. Benedict is your uncle." But even as he said the words his voice faltered. Suddenly he wasn't so confident.

"Benedict is not my uncle," she said evenly. "We just say that he is. It sounds better that we are related. After all, our magic is inherited."

Pin staggered and sank to the ground, his head in his hands. "Oh Juno, I'm so sorry. I should have trusted you. But what was I supposed to think? My mother was buried with a silver locket, her last piece of jewelry." He looked up in despair. "Why are you here? What are you digging for?"

"Pin," said Juno slowly, "I've got to tell you the truth."

"The truth? What do you mean? I know everything. Just give me another chance. We can still go together. You can be the Bone Magician and I'll be your assistant—"

"Stop," commanded Juno, and Pin froze. "I want you to

come with me, of course I do, but you have to know something first. I'm here because I was trying to put something back. I know it was stupid, idiotic, but I had to try. I couldn't live with myself otherwise." She picked up the brown bag and offered it to Pin.

"This is yours, by right."

Slowly and with shaking hands Pin took the bag. He knelt on the ground and pulled apart the strings and turned it upside down. There tumbled out before him a pile of dry bones. But still he didn't understand. And there was something else, a brown skull, with wispy hair, that rolled out and stopped at his feet.

"Madame de Bona?" he whispered.

"No," said Juno. "Your mother."

CHAPTER THIRTY,NINE

Juno Tells a Story

Pin looked up in utter bewilderment. His stomach lurched. He thought he might be sick.

"My mother? But how?"

"Let me tell you . . ."

My mother died when I was very young. I have no memory of her at all, it was my father who brought me up. He was a physician in a town not far from here. He did well enough, and he taught me everything he knew. About the healing properties of herbs and spices. About how to make unguents and tonics and potions, how to apply cups and leeches. And he showed me how to make the *Credo* potion, the one I use at the raisings. You're right to think it's the key. It's a suggestible potion, you see. It frees the mind to see what it wants to see. All you have to do is focus on what you wish for and when you inhale the potion, it allows you to experience your dreams. Only for a little while, though, but long enough. All those people who came to see Madame de Bona, in their hearts they wanted to believe that she could come back to life. And because that's what they desired, that's what they got. As for their questions, they already knew the answers they wanted, but it felt better to hear them from someone else, even if it was a skeleton. You're right about the juniper unguent in the locket too. It protects you from the *Credo* potion.

"Anyway, we did well enough. People were grateful to my father for curing their ills and they paid him good money. They even left him some when they died. But then a rumor started that he had become greedy, that he was killing people for their money. And not long after that he was murdered, by trickery.

"Of course everything changed for me then. People began to say that I might have had a hand in my father's scheming, and life became impossible. You know how it is to be treated like a criminal even when you are innocent. I suffered in the same way. So I left the town and came to Urbs Umida. I found out soon enough that it is a lonely and cruel place and I did not fare too well. I had taken to sheltering in the churchyard at night. I felt safe there. Pickpockets and thieves tend to ply their trade among the living, not the dead. As for grave robbers and body snatchers, well, they were too busy to take any notice of a pauper girl trying to sleep. When I first saw Benedict I thought he was just another one of them. I came upon him, digging up a grave, toward the end of last summer."

"My mother's?" said Pin softly and Juno nodded.

"'If you're looking for a body, then that's the wrong grave,' I said to him. 'Been dead six months. It'll only be bones.'

"'That's what I want,' he said.

"'Bones? What do you want bones for?'

"He stood up and looked at me. I could tell that he was old, too old for digging.

"'You look like a strong lass,' he said. 'Help me out here. This'll be the death of me.'

"I didn't move. He understood well enough. We agreed on a shilling and I took the spade. It wasn't that hard. The ground was soft after a rainfall, the earth was loose enough, and he'd done most of the work already. It wasn't long before I had the coffin unearthed. And I was right, only bones. Benedict seemed pleased."

"What about her locket?" asked Pin suddenly.

"There was nothing, believe me," said Juno softly. "I swear it. I think that perhaps the grave had already been robbed. The coffin lid was not nailed down." She looked at Pin. "Is this too much for you? Do you want me to stop?"

He shook his head. "No, I want to know everything."

"Well, Benedict put the bones into the bag and made ready to go. I was intrigued and I asked him what he was going to do with them. He said that he had thought of a way to make money. He was going to travel with the skeleton and exhibit her as a sort of soothsayer who could tell fortunes.

" 'And how is she going to do that?' I asked. 'She is dead.'

" 'I thought perhaps I could throw my voice,' he said.

"I laughed. I told him the whole idea was preposterous and that it could never work.

"Benedict was a little put out. 'Do you have a better idea?'

" 'In fact I do,' I said and I told him about the *Credo* potion. I was certain that we could use it to our advantage. Together Benedict and I hatched our plan. He would be the Bone Magician and I would make the potion and do the voices. That's why I wore such a long hood, so people couldn't see that Madame de Bona's voice was actually mine. No one was looking at me anyway. We left the City and traveled all over the country. It suited me well enough. We made money, especially from private raisings, and as we went from place to place I made inquiries about the man who murdered my father. And sometimes, just once or twice, we were close to him, but always we were too late."

"But what about all the questions?" asked Pin. "How did you know what to say?"

Juno smiled. "I became quite skilled at answering questions without actually saying anything. You should know, Pin. You asked Madame de Bona about your father. I hardly told you anything helpful, but when you're under the influence of the *Credo* potion, anything I say sounds plausible. All those exhortations to Hades, master of the shades of the dead. It means nothing. It's all for show. The only thing that really matters is the potion.

"But things have changed. Benedict's health started to fail and I still hadn't found the man I was looking for. And other things were troubling me too. I began to feel that what we were doing wasn't right. When I heard the same questions being asked of Madame de Bona over and over again, I realized that I was cheating these people, influencing their minds with my potion and telling them what they wanted to hear, lies disguised as the truth. I said to Benedict that I didn't want to do any more private raisings and we agreed that Sybil would be the last one. Mr. Belding wasn't just a curious spectator who came to be entertained. He was a desperate man. That was the hardest thing I have ever done, maybe the cruelest, pretending to forgive him."

"Is that why you don't want to take Madame de Bona with you when you leave the City?" asked Pin. He couldn't bring himself to say "my mother."

"Partly," said Juno. "But I only made my mind up for definite tonight, when I saw the white flower in your handkerchief. You said you found it on your mother's grave."

Pin nodded slowly. "But what's that got to do with anything?"

By now Juno was speaking between wrenching sobs. "You see, Pin, I put the flowers on her grave, only I didn't know who she was then. When I found out tonight I couldn't believe what I had done. How could I take Madame de Bona, *your mother*, with me after that? I decided to leave without you—cowardly, I know, but I was in shock. I've tried to make it right, to put her back. But I can't. The ground is too hard."

Juno looked at Pin through glassy, red-rimmed eyes. "Can you ever forgive me?" she whispered. "It's a terrible thing I've done."

Pin stood up shakily and went to Juno and put his arms around her. "Of course I forgive you. I can't say it doesn't hurt, but you didn't know. And you were trying to make things right."

"Here," said Juno. She handed him a bouquet of dried white flowers. "Daisies from the Moiraean Mountains. I was going to put them in the coffin. They mean 'sorry.' "

CHAPTER FORTY

Article from

The Urbs Umida Daily Chronicle

SILVER APPLE KILLER UNCOVERED
BY
DEODONATUS SNOAD

My Dear Readers,

I am sure that by now there are very few of you out there who have not heard of the escape of the Gluttonous Beast. At this point in time I cannot comment on his whereabouts or his intentions, but no doubt you will find these out for yourselves soon enough.

There is every possibility you also know that it was I, Deodonatus Snoad, who released the Beast. Perhaps it was Mr. Idolice who told you. I wonder: did he also tell you how he kept *me* in captivity for eight years in his traveling circus, Rudy Idolice's Peregrinating Panopticon of Wonders, and showed me under the name of Mr. Hideous? I suffered daily, as did the Beast, the torment of being poked and prodded and stared at. But, unlike the Beast, I was able to break free and to pursue my life as I wished. Perhaps now you begin to understand why I would do such a thing as to allow a Beast of wholly unrestrained temperament to roam free in the City. All I will have done is to afford him the same opportunity as I had, and I am sure that he will be grateful for it. Of course, there is always the possibility that you will not even notice him among you, such is the nature of this city.

There is one other thing I can reveal on this page, my final piece for the *Chronicle*. I am quite certain that this is a fact not yet in your possession: the identity of the Silver Apple Killer. I can divulge this to you now because I intend to be far away from Urbs Umida when you read this. Like the Beast, I will start a new life.

You see, my Dear Readers—and I mean that with the utmost sincerity, as I realize now that you have in your own way been my only friends these past few years—I, Deodonatus Snoad, your humble servant in all newsworthy matters of this city, am the Silver Apple Killer.

"But why?" I hear you cry. "What have we done to deserve this?"

Well, let me tell you. *You went to gaze upon the Beast.* That is what you did.

At least I am not like him, you thought, as you stared heartlessly at him in his cage. And then you walked out onto the Bridge and wondered why you were struck down. And now the Beast is free to take his own revenge. Perhaps he has already. And it is no more than you deserve, every gawking one of you.

Remember,

Ὁ ανόητον θεωρεῖ ανόητο ως καλόν·

There will be no next time,

Deodonatus Snoad

Note from the Editor:

This piece was delivered to the offices of the *Chronicle* the same night the Beast was released. Bearing in mind the subject of the article, we considered that you, the people of Urbs Umida, should have the opportunity to read it. Unfortunately, there is no news of the Beast as yet. We can only hope that he is captured before anyone else comes to any harm. As for Deodonatus Snoad, he was found dead, along with Rudy Idolice, locked inside the Beast's cage the morning following its release. We can only speculate that the Beast was not as grateful for his freedom as Deodonatus might have wished.

The Editor

P.S. As far as we can make out, the Greek quotation means:

"An ass thinks an ass a pretty fellow."

Make of it what you will.

CHAPTER FORTY-ONE

Pin's Journal

Well, Dear Reader (as Deodonatus was so fond of saying, although I do not suppose so many will ever read this journal as read the "Chronicle"), I cannot say when I will be writing again. We are packed and ready to go, Juno and I, and we have said our good-byes. I shall not miss Urbs Umida, but I shall miss Squid's Gate Alley, where we leave some good friends: Benedict and Aluph—to whom I gave for safekeeping my mother's bones—Beag, and Mrs. Hoadswood, who has sustained us with her cooking in this miserable place. We gratefully take some with us in our bags.

We have all read the "Chronicle." Aluph is certain that Deodonatus was trying to tell us through his writings that he was the Silver Apple Killer. His mistake, however, was to talk about fault. There is not a soul in this city who would ever accept that they might be to blame for something. It is not in their nature! Aluph was most concerned about Mr. Snoad's Friction Stick, but there was not a trace of it to be found, neither in his lodging house nor at the Nimble Finger. No doubt it will surface eventually.

The only thing of interest that was found at Deodonatus's lodgings was a copy of "Houndsecker's Tales of Faeries and Blythe Spirits." Deodonatus seemed well acquainted with the tale of the princess and the toad. It explained a lot.

CHAPTER FORTY TWO

Departure

$\mathfrak{I}$t was late afternoon when Juno and Pin walked briskly over the Bridge toward the city gates on the other side of the river. Beneath them once again the Foedus was making slow progress inland, groaning and creaking with her burden of broken ice and colorful debris from the stalls that had traded on her frozen back. The thaw had started the previous evening and the streets once more were slushy streams of muck and the smell of the river was heavy in the air. Pin breathed deeply and Juno laughed.

"I should have thought you would be glad to get that smell out of your head."

Pin smiled. "It is a smell I will never forget," he said. "And it will always remind me of everything that happened in this city." He put his hand to his collar and felt for the tiny bone, the tip of his mother's little finger, that was hanging from a string around his neck.

"I think I prefer my smells," said Juno, laughing.

"Well, it's all behind us now," said Pin. "And who knows what's ahead?"

"The truth, perhaps," said Juno, thoughtfully, "about your father."

"Maybe," said Pin. "Though sometimes the truth isn't such a great thing after all. And what about you? This man you are looking for, what will you do if you find him?"

"He has something that belonged to my father," said Juno. "I will ask for it back."

"And what's that?"

"A wooden leg."

"Do you know his name?"

"I do," said Juno. "His name is Joe Zabbidou."

A Note from F. E. Higgins

So it appears that we have reached the end, and what an end! After uncovering a seemingly unrelated cast of characters in Urbs Umida, once again I was led back to Joe Zabbidou. I keep Pin's box—waxed and polished—beside the wooden leg. I know somehow they are both connected. And in more ways than one. Those of you with sharp memories might recall that there was a confession in Joe Zabbidou's Black Book that started thus: "My name is Oscar Carpue. In a fit of mindless rage, gripped by madness, I..."

This, of course, begs the question—one of many—did Pin's father kill Fabian or didn't he? And will Juno Catchpole ever find Joe Zabbidou? As yet, I do not have the answers. Having come this far, how could I not continue!

In the words of Deodonatus Snoad,

Until next time...

F. E. Higgins
Urbs Umida

Appendix I

The Princess and the Toad
from *Houndsecker's Tales of Faeries and Blythe Spirits*

I thought this might shed some light on the complicated nature of Deodonatus Snoad's thinking and the meaning of the silver apple.—Author

There was once a beautiful princess who had everything a princess could wish for. Beauty and wealth, and a loving father and mother. She lived in a marvelous castle and spent her days playing in the surrounding gardens. She was a kind princess, but she had one fault. She suffered somewhat from pride. Her father warned her on many occasions that one day her pride would teach her a lesson.

"I am sure you are right," she said gaily, but she paid him little heed and ran away.

It happened one day that she was playing in the rose garden south of the castle. She liked to play there because the ground was mossy and springy under her feet and in the center of the grass there was an ancient well. When she became hot she would wind down the bucket and draw up some of the cool clear water that lay deep below to splash on her face.

On that particular day, she saw something glittering in the grass. She reached down and recovered a small silver apple, just big enough to fit into the palm of her hand. In the sunlight it was quite beautiful and she threw it into the air and delighted in catching it. Then she threw it so high that she lost sight of it in the brightness of the sun, only to hear a moment later a loud splash from within the well.

She ran over to the well and looked into the darkness, but there was no sign of it. But she was not one to give up so easily. *Perhaps,* she mused, *there is a way.*

Carefully she lowered the bucket into the water and then brought it up again full to the brim. Hopefully she peered inside and exclaimed with joy when she saw something glistening at the bottom. Quickly she emptied it, but it was not a silver apple that sat before her, only a gleaming toad. Its green legs were splayed on the grass and its toes gripped the mossy ground. Its knobbly skin and wide grin repulsed her.

"Ugh," she exclaimed and turned her head away.

"Please don't turn away from me," said a voice, and when the princess looked again through her fingers, she saw that it was indeed the toad that was speaking.

"Why not?" she demanded. "You are too ugly to deserve my gaze."

The toad looked up at her sadly. "I might be able to help you," he said.

The princess laughed, rather nastily. "And what could you do for me?"

"I could fetch your silver apple," he said. "It is at the bottom of the well. If you could just put me in the bucket and lower me down, I can get it for you."

"But I would have to touch your ugly skin," she said.

"Is that such a torment for you?" asked the toad, and the princess thought of the beautiful silver apple and said, "Perhaps not. But I shall have to close my eyes."

"Very well, if that is your wish," said the toad, good-naturedly.

"And once you have recovered my silver apple," said the princess, "then that will be the end of it?"

The toad cocked its head to one side. "I ask only one thing," it said, "in return for my help."

"And that is?" The princess looked surprised. After all, what favor could she possibly do the toad?

"As soon as the apple is in your hands, you must kiss me."

The princess could hardly keep the look of disgust from her face, but such was her desire for the apple that she agreed all the same. So she closed her eyes, picked up the toad, all the time grimacing, and dropped it quite harshly into the bucket before lowering it into the well.

"I have it," called the toad from the bottom of the well,

and the princess began to pull up the bucket. As it came nearer and nearer she regretted her rash promise and cruelly let the bucket go. It rattled all the way down and hit the water with a loud splash. The princess ignored the toad's cries and ran back to the castle.

That night there was a terrible storm with torrential rain. The next morning the princess went back to the rose garden as usual, but when she saw the well she gasped, for it was overflowing with water and there, sitting on the grass, was the toad with the silver apple between its feet.

"The rain has lifted me out of the well," he said. "It was so unfortunate that you dropped the bucket yesterday."

The princess, sensitive to the toad's good nature, felt dreadful remorse at the way she had treated him.

"Would you like the silver apple?"

"I would indeed," she said, "but first I must do something for you." She bent down and kissed him gently on the cheek. And lo and behold when she opened her eyes again the toad was gone, and in his place stood a handsome prince.

Appendix II

The Shaking Spider
Pholcus phalangioides

Also known as the daddy longlegs spider, *Pholcus* usually remains perfectly still in its web during the day. When disturbed, however, it shakes itself vigorously up and down, causing the web to vibrate along with it, to ward off predators. *Pholcus's* long legs are an advantage because they allow the spider to keep well away from dangerous prey while simultaneously flicking spinnerets at it to bind it up. *Pholcus* feeds on insects and other spiders, even its own kind. At night the males search out females and make their presence known by gently vibrating the web. Initially the hatched spiderlings stay around the mother's web, but as they grow they move away to avoid being eaten by their siblings.